The Trackers of Oxyrhynchus

THE
TRACKERS
OF
OXYRHYNCHUS

The Delphi Text 1988

TONY HARRISON

faber and faber

LONDON · BOSTON

First published in 1990
by Faber and Faber Limited
3 Queen Square London WC1N 3AU

Photoset by Goodfellow & Egan Ltd, Cambridge
Printed in Great Britain by Richard Clay Ltd, Bungay, Suffolk

ISBN 0–571–15496–4

CONTENTS

Introduction   vii

The Trackers of Oxyrhynchus   I

Appendix: Music Samples   73

INTRODUCTION

One

Something prepared me for Greek drama long before I knew a word of ancient Greek, or had ever heard the names of Hecuba or Oedipus. It began with the creation of what I call my 'orchestra' in the sense I later learned for that Greek word meaning 'circular dancing place'. This 'orchestra' became my first brooding ground and, I think, the first intimation of what for me is the basic struggle of art. I was eight. We were celebrating what was called VJ (Victory over Japan) night with a large bonfire in the back street outside our house. The atmosphere was more celebratory than I can ever remember before or since, with normally taciturn people laughing, singing, dancing at the end of a terrible war. Furniture was brought out of houses to keep the blaze going. The fire became so high the telephone wires were burned down. The paint on our back gate blistered and peeled off. It went on all night and in the morning I helped to douse the fire and shovel the ashes into tea chests to be taken away. When the space was cleared the celebratory bonfire had left a black circle of scorched cobbles with thick scars of tar.

Forty-five years later the circle is still there. Looking into that circle I once thought of it as the nightsky globe totally devoid of stars, an annihilated universe. It was something like Byron's vision in 'Darkness':

> I had a dream, which was not all a dream,
> The bright sun was extinguished, and the stars
> Did wander darkling in the eternal space . . .

It looked like this when my imagination couldn't cope with the twentieth century. It was in this starless shape, even before I became a poet, that I learned to relate our celebratory fire, with the white-hot coils from domestic sofas, to that terrible form of fire that brought about the 'VJ' when unleashed on Hiroshima and Nagasaki in August 1945. One element for celebration and terror. One space for the celebrant and the sufferer.

I began to learn to people that scorched orchestra only after an immersion in the drama of the ancient Greeks. Things just as 'dark' occurred in this orchestra of Dionysus but it was lit by the sun and was surrounded by a community as bonded in their watching as we had been by our celebratory blaze. It was a drama open-eyed about suffering but with a heart still open to celebration and physical affirmation. In the late twentieth century, what clues to existential survival could be found in an ancient drama which managed to face up to the worst things it could imagine and yet not banish the celebratory? What style permitted the sufferer and the celebrant to share the same space? What were the ways and means?

Though the texts of ancient drama are constantly annotated and re-annotated, some of the factors I have found essential to the drama's affirmation are often overlooked.

The first thing to observe about Greek drama is that it was staged in the common light of day. A shared space and a shared light. Our word 'theatre' is derived from the Greek word θεατρον, a place of seeing. Not only did the audience (Φεατες: 'those who see' in Greek) *see* the action of tragedy, not only did the audience *see* the actors and chorus but the actors and chorus *saw* the audience. They were all equally illuminated by the light of the sun. The lighting grid was the great globe itself. In Athens of the fifth century BC that 'obvious reciprocity', that Harbage found between actors and audience in Shakespeare's theatre, was created from the beginning of the experience by the shared space and shared light. When Bertolt Brecht writes in one of his theatre poems, *The Lighting*

Give us some light on the stage, electrician. How can we
Playwrights and actors put forward
Our images of the world in half darkness? The dim twilight
Induces sleep. But we need the audience's
Wakeful-, even watchful-ness. Let them
Do their dreaming in the light.

viii

and when Yeats writes that in the theatre 'the essential thing is always full or almost full light because the actor comes first', and how he would like to compel a theatrical producer to 'produce some Shakespearian play with all the stage lights in every scene', applying that principle even to the storm scene in *King Lear*; when Peter Brook brought the houselights up at the end of the first act of *King Lear*, before the blinding of Gloucester; when Poel looked for a lighting which 'evoked the open air'; and when Granville Barker's plans for an 'exemplary theatre' included 'provisions for performing in daylight', a suggestion his biographer calls 'wonderfully radical', when all these men of the theatre made these statements and gestures, they were expressing, in their various ways, a deep nostalgia for the theatre of daylight.

The Greeks had no need of a lighting system to 'evoke the open air'. They had such a system in the sun, which linked audience and performers in a common light. There was no atmospheric darkening of the stage for illusionary effect, nor to conceal such a spectacle as the Oedipus with gouged eye-sockets. Voltaire's suggestion in his note to Corneille's preface to *Oedipe*, that dim lighting might make that terrible image tolerable, would make no sense to Sophocles, who has the blinded king described as a 'spectacle', something to be looked at, a θεαμα, from the same root of the verb 'to see', that gives us theatre. It is also as a 'spectacle', in the same Greek word, that Prometheus draws attention to himself and the injustice he suffers at the hands of Zeus. His final cry is to the 'common light' that unites actor and audience, theatrical space and outside world, the imaginary and the real.

This 'light common to all' (παντων κοινον φαος, *Prometheus Bound* 1091–2) is the first essential of ancient drama. The light is the first thing to be addressed by Prometheus or Alcestis or Ion and it is not only the illumination in the sense of the lighting that unites audience and performer in a shared experience but also in the sense of spiritual understanding. Things are brought, as Oedipus says 'εις το φως', to the light, or as we might say, 'to the light of day'. Shared space and shared light. How different from the darkened auditoria of our day.

A Greek theatrical mask is part of the existential survival gear. It gives the bearing of survival to the actor wearing it. It represents a commitment to seeing everything through the eyes that never close. It represents a commitment to going on speaking when the always open eyes have witnessed something unspeakable. The masks must witness the unendurable. That is why they are created with their eyes open. The mouth must continue to speak in situations where the human being would be speechless or screaming and unable to articulate its agony. The shared space and light allow this seeing and this speaking. The shared light begs a common language. The mask is always 'presented'. It sees the audience looking at it. It seems to see more people than a human eye. A chorus of masks patrols the attention of the audience. If you know you are seen you know you are being addressed, and you attend.

The space and light and the mask are created for a communal act of attention, a deep concentration in which the spellbinding metrical language also plays a primary part. Performability is not something injected afterwards into a text. Greek texts are created with the performability for that known space in the conditions of shared light, and created to be spoken in masks to an audience that is *seen* and never cut off in darkened seats. Above all, since the expression 'to see the light' in Greek means to live, the final sense is that of shared *life*. And it is to that life that the masked upright figure of Hecuba commits herself and us at the very end of *The Trojan Women* of Euripides, and not to the 'total nihilism' that Sartre found in the play.

But even that commitment to life was not the end of the drama. The broken Trojan refugees were not the final image. After every third play in a group of three tragedies, as *The Trojan Women* was, would come a satyr play written by the same author, with a chorus of what we can see as men in their animal condition, represented as half or three quarters man with horse or goat attributes and an erect phallus. The unease that is felt and has long been felt at the idea of the bloated celebrant following hard on the heels of the sufferer has been responsible, along with natural oblivion, for the loss of these plays, which amount to a quarter of the whole large output of the great dramatists, Aeschylus, Sophocles and Euripides.

With the loss of these plays we are lacking important clues to the wholeness of the Greek imagination, and its ability to absorb and yet not be defeated by the tragic. In the satyr play, that spirit of celebration, held in the dark solution of tragedy, is precipitated into release, and a release into the worship of the Dionysus who presided over the whole dramatic festival. In the one complete surviving satyr play, the *Cyclops* of Euripides, the very last line allows the chorus the prospect of being liberated finally from the dark shadow of the Cyclops Polyphemus and spend the rest of the time in the service of Bacchus. This journey back into the service of the presiding god seems to be paralleled by the release of the spirit back to the life of the senses at the end of the tragic journey. It is unlikely that the quaffing promised to the Dionysian band was one in which a drop was taken from the cup for the sufferers of the preceding tragedy, as at Passover one drop of wine is removed from the cup of joy for each of the ten plagues which befell Egypt at the time of the exodus, but the sensual relish for life and its affirmation must have been the spirit of the conclusion of the four plays. The satyrs are included in the wholeness of the tragic vision. They are not forgotten or forced out by pseudo 'refinement'.

Without the satyr play we cannot know enough about the way in which the Greek spirit coped with catastrophe. The residue of a few tragedies might give us the illusion of something resolutely high-minded but it is a distortion, with which post-Christian culture has been more comfortable than with the whole picture. The thought of tragedy and satyrs co-existing has not been easy even for the most comprehensive of scholars. Even Sir Arthur Pickard-Cambridge, to whom we are all indebted for the description of the material environment of Greek drama, has a problem characteristic of the scholarship on it:

> The problem which if baffling to modern and Christian readers – how it was possible for the same audience, possibly even on the same day, to be absorbed in the noblest tragedy

and pass immediately to the grossness, which . . . comedy displayed for at least a century and a half – would not have been appreciated by the Athenians of the fifth century, and it is one which will never be completely solved.

The stress on Christian and *readers* helps us to understand the problem. Christianity, with what D.H. Lawrence called 'its lust for the end of the world', certainly drove a wedge into human nature and subverted the wholeness of an earlier imagination. The shrivelled private scope of readership rather than presence in shared light and space made both parts of the Greek spirit harder to accommodate. The essential catholicity of Greek drama, the unity of tragedy and satyr play, has been betrayed into divided and divisive categories, 'high' and 'low'. The Byzantine compilers helped to initiate this process by choosing only few representative tragedies for study. Discoveries outside of this ancient selection include those plays that help to undermine the view of drama as uniformly high-minded, even, given its early period of history, straining for an acceptable monotheistic maturity! The so-called 'alphabet' plays of Euripides included not only the one surviving satyr play but also the category-disturbing *Alcestis*, often termed 'proto-satyric' because Euripides offered it in place of the satyr play as the fourth play of his competition entry. In this play Euripides introduced his 'satyr', in the shape of Herakles, into the very body of the tragedy: the celebrant admitted before the tragic section had come to an end. The playwright thus showed both elements interwined, doing what Johnson said of Shakespeare, depicting neither 'tragedy' nor 'comedy' but the real state of 'sublunary nature' in which '*at the same time* the reveler is hasting to his wine and the mourner is burying his friend', or, in the case of Herakles in *Alcestis*, getting drunk while Admetus is burying his wife. It is, of course, precisely this quality in Shakespeare that has given those who want their genius more 'refined' the same problems that classicists have had with Greek drama. One such characteristic voice was that of Robert Bridges, Poet Laureate from 1913 to 1930:

Shakespeare should not be put into the hands of the young without the warning that the foolish things in his plays were written to please the foolish, the filthy for the filthy, and the brutal for the brutal; and that if out of our veneration for his genius we are led to admire or even tolerate such things, we may be thereby not conforming ourselves to him, but only degrading ourselves to the level of his audience, and learning contamination from those wretched beings who can never be forgiven their share in preventing the greatest poet and dramatist of the world from being the best artist.

How far we already are from that shared space and light of the Greeks. The divided art is perpetuating divided audiences, divided societies. This audience of Shakespeare's time, so despised and patronized by the Poet Laureate, is exactly the same as that which Alfred Harbage thought should take some of the credit for the greatness of Shakespeare's plays. It was due in part to that 'obvious reciprocity' which also existed abundantly in ancient Athens. Harbage's account of the audience in Shakespeare's theatre immediately shows up all that is throughly undemocratic in the view of Bridges.

Mere coincidence will not explain why every Elizabethan play addressed to a *sector* of the people, high or low, learned or unlearned, is inferior in quality; why neither university nor law school, nor guild hall, nor princely banquet house begat dramatic poetry comparable to what came from the public theatres; or why Blackfriars failed to sustain the level achieved by the Globe. The drama reached its peak when the audience formed *a great amalgam*, and it began its decline when the amalgam was split in two.

If we stress the 'free' and the 'men' of 'freemen of Athens' we have a similar 'great amalgam' in ancient Athens, despite the fact it seems highly likely that slaves and even women were not at the theatres. A recent survey has shown that modern theatre audiences are composed of élite and privileged *sectors* of our society. For two of the greatest moments in world drama it seems to have been otherwise. W.B. Stanford has shown that the Athenian audiences were not simply intellectuals and sophisticated citizens but 'farmers, craftsmen, shopkeepers, manual labourers in far greater numbers than the priests, poets, philosophers and sophists'. He tells us that we should do well to remember that when it came to voting for the groups of four plays submitted in the competition the vote of a shoemaker was as good as a vote from a philosopher. The social composition of the audience in that shared space and shared light was not only a 'great amalgam' but could see that it was. Those gathered together had that kind of recognition of each other as belonging to the same society, but would only gather together on these important festival occasions; the uniqueness of the event also united them. We might say that TV reaches such an amalgam, but it is not present in the same space: TV viewers are not aware of each other attending, and therefore sharing not only the space and the light, but the illumination in the spiritual sense. When drama lost those conditions it became less able to bear and digest the worst things it could imagine. Dramas became texts divided into 'high' and 'low' art. The loss of satyr plays is both a symptom and a consequence of this division. What is lost is a clue to the wholeness of the Greek imagination and its deep compulsion to unite sufferer and celebrant in the same space and light. In the end those who feel excluded from 'high' art and relegated to 'low' will sooner or later want to destroy what they are not allowed to inhabit.

If we have a nostalgia for the theatre of daylight it is a sign of regret for a culture where the celebrant is born out of tragedy before our eyes. With us the masque and the anti-masque are as divided, as they were when Shelley saw that division as both the 'sign and the thing signified' in his regrettably uncompleted drama *Charles I* of 1819:

> Ay, there they are –
> Nobles, and sons of nobles, patentees,
> Monopolists, and stewards of this poor farm,
> On whose lean sheep sit the prophetic crows,
> Here is the pomp that strips the houseless orphan,
> Here is the pride that breaks the desolate heart.

These are not the lilies glorious as Solomon,
Who toil not, neither do they spin, – unless
It be the webs they catch poor rogues withal.
Here is the surfeit which to them who earn
The niggard wages of the earth, scarce leaves
The tithe that will support them till they crawl
Back to her cold hard bosom. Here is health
Followed by grim disease, glory by shame,
Waste by lame famine, wealth by squalid want,
And England's sin by England's punishment.
And, as the effect pursues the cause foregone,
Lo, giving substance to my words, behold
At once the sign and the thing signified –
A troop of cripples, beggars, and lean outcasts,
Horsed upon stumbling jades, carted with dung,
Dragged for a day from cellars and low cabins
And rotten hiding-holes, to point the moral
Of this presentiment, and bring up the rear
Of painted pomp with misery!

THE YOUTH

'Tis but

The anti-masque, and serves as discords do
In sweeter music. Who would love May flowers
If they succeeded not to Winter's flaw;
Or day unchanged by night; or joy itself
Without the touch of sorrow?

SECOND CITIZEN

I and thou –

A MARSHALSMAN

Place, give place!

And the Marshalsmen of division go on crying 'place, give
place' in all our palaces of culture still.

Two

In 1907 Grenfell & Hunt, the Holmes and Watson of Oxford
papyrology, discovered the tattered remains of a lost satyr play

of Sophocles, the *Ichneutae* ('The Trackers'). The discovery of the papyrus with some 400 incomplete lines was announced at the Annual General Meeting of the Egypt Exploration Society by Dr Hunt, in the following words:

. . . Three years ago we were indebted to Oxyrhynchus for some extensive remains of a lost tragedy of Euripides, the *Hypsipyle*. It is now the turn of Sophocles; and most fortunately the discovery to which I refer represents a side of the poet concerning which we have been very much in the dark. As you know, it was customary to produce tragedies in trilogies, or sets of three, which were followed by a Satyric drama, a lighter piece in which the chorus consisted of Satyrs, and the high tension of the preceding tragedies was relaxed. Only one specimen of such a Satyric drama has come down to us, the *Cyclops* of Euripides. Of the work of Sophocles, as of Aeschylus, in this line there exist only short disjointed fragments preserved in citations by grammarians and others. I am glad to say that for Sophocles what may be considered a fair sample is now recovered.

When found, the papyrus in question was, as usual, much broken up; in fact, the various fragments were not even all obtained in the same year. But they have fitted together remarkably well, and as now arranged make up the first sixteen columns of the play, accounting for over 400 lines, of which about one half are complete or easily completed, and many more sufficiently well preserved to be intelligible. Since the length of a Satyric drama seems to have been considerably less than that of the ordinary tragedy, the amount recovered may well represent as much as half of the original whole. The play is the *Ichneutae*, or 'The Trackers', of which practically nothing beyond the title was previously known. It is based upon the familiar myth of the exploits of the infant god Hermes – his theft of Apollo's cattle and his invention of the lyre. Apollo, in an opening speech, announces the loss of the cattle, for which he has vainly sought, and offers rewards to the finder. Silenus then appears with his attendant Satyrs, and proposes to join in the search.

Encouraged by Silenus, the chorus start out on the quest – they are the 'Trackers' from whom the play is named. They soon discover traces of the cattle, leading to the entrance of a cave; but here they are alarmed by curious sounds which they do not understand – the notes of the newly-invented lyre with which Hermes is amusing himself down below. Silenus upbraids them for their timidity, and at length himself knocks at the barrier, and a nymph emerges. In answer to their questions, she explains that she is the nurse of the child who has been lately born to Zeus, and whose abnormal growth is so startling, and tells them of his invention of the lyre. But she stoutly defends him against the imputation of being concerned in the theft. They remain unconvinced; some cowhide admittedly has been used in making the lyre, and there are tell-tale tracks on the ground. While the dispute is in progress Apollo returns, and accepts the evidence offered by Silenus and the Satyrs as entitling them to the promised reward. Here the papyrus breaks off; no doubt in the sequel Hermes appeared on the scene and appeased Apollo by the gift of the lyre, as narrated in the Homeric hymn.

The piece was thus slight enough. Like the *Cyclops* of Euripides, it is a short and simple dramatisation of a well-known story, to which a Satyric setting was appropriate. An element of comedy was supplied by the grotesque figures of Silenus and the chorus, whose imitation of dogs upon the scent lends itself to some rather broad humour. While bearing the unmistakable Sophoclean stamp, this play thus differs entirely in theme and treatment from the other plays of Sophocles which we possess; and it fills up to some extent a gap in our knowledge of the dramatist's art.

Three

As Dr Hunt says, we can probably assume that in the gaps of the papyrus Hermes appeared and appeased Apollo by the gift of the lyre, and certainly in the Homeric *Hymn to Hermes* the infant inventor makes a mollifying benefaction to the god. The story goes as follows in Shelley's version of the hymn:

LXXXII

'Thou canst seek out and compass all that wit
    Can find or teach; – yet since thou wilt, come take
The lyre – be mine the glory giving it –
    Strike the sweet chords, and sing aloud, and wake
The joyous pleasure out of many a fit
    Of tranced sound – and with fleet fingers make
Thy liquid-voiced comrade talk with thee, –
It can talk measured music eloquently.

LXXXII

'Then bear it boldly to the revel loud,
    Love-wakening dance, or feast of solemn state,
A joy by night or day – for those endowed
    With art and wisdom who interrogate
It teaches, babbling in delightful mood
    All things which make the spirit most elate,
Soothing the mind with sweet familiar play,
Chasing the heavy shadows of dismay.

LXXXIII

'To those who are unskilled in its sweet tongue,
    Though they should question most impetuously
Its hidden soul, it gossips something wrong –
    Some senseless and impertinent reply.
But thou who art as wise as thou art strong
    Canst compass all that thou desirest. I
Present thee with this music-flowing shell,
Knowing thou canst interrogate it well.

LXXXIV

'And let us two henceforth together feed
    On this green mountain slope and pastoral plain,
The herds in litigation – they will breed
    Quickly enough to recompense our pain,

xviii

If to the bulls and cows we take good heed; –
   And thou, though somewhat over fond of gain,
   Grudge me not half the profit.' Having spoke
   The shell he proffered, and Apollo took.

But there is an alternative version to this story of the tranquil takeover of the lyre, just as there is an alternative version of the story of the peaceful transition of the shrine of Delphi from Gaia to Apollo as told, for example, in the *Oresteia*. In some stories Apollo bludgeoned his way into possessing what was once a female shrine 'And Apollo took'! In the Valley of the Muses, near Askra, the birthplace of Hesiod, in Euboea, which I visited in 1987, and again after the première of *The Trackers of Oxyrhynchus*, there was once, according to Pausanias, who saw it, a bronze of Apollo and Hermes *fighting* for the lyre.

In these thorn-strewn slopes leading up to the summit of Helicon there were not only statues to the Muses, looted by Constantine, and the one mentioned by Pausanias representing the struggle of Apollo and Hermes for the lyre. There were also other cautionary bronzes. There was a statue of Thamyris shown blind, with his lyre shattered at his feet. He was blinded for his presumption in offering competition on the lyre. Near by was a statue of Linus, killed by Apollo for offering him rivalry in singing. Pausanias doesn't mention that there was a bronze of Marsyas, the satyr, flayed alive for competing on the flute against Apollo's lyre. For the divine patron of music and poetry, the Parnassian supremo, this is appalling savagery, but this pugnacity and paranoid possessiveness are characteristic of Apollo's early transition from macho cowpoke to cultural impresario. Rival lyre players, singers, upstart satyr flautists, flayed, butchered, blinded, were set up as deterrents in the Valley of the Muses and elsewhere. Herodotus says that the skin of Marsyas was pegged out in a public square in Celaenae (in what is now Turkey) and though it vibrated sympathetically to any Phrygian air, remained stubbornly silent when hymns in praise of Apollo were played in its vicinity. We are told that Apollo had the flute of Marsyas hung up as a trophy in his temple at Sicyon in the Peloponnese. Apollo was only reconciled to the flute he always abhorred after his competition with Marsyas, when it was used by the flute player Sakadas to play a hymn to the god in Delphi. Flute-players are admitted if they play the Paean to Apollo. It seems that the flute of Marsyas did not show the same loyalty to its first animator as the 'the auld Orange Flute' or indeed the skin flayed from the flautist himself.

The Roman emperors Augustus and Nero both loved to dress up as Apollo and it was probably the lyre of Apollo that Nero 'fiddled' on while Rome went up in flames, a cool behaviour long endorsed by Apollo himself. A few months ago in Nicosia I saw a sign saying 'Apollo: Quality Underwear' and I suppose the Y-front endorsement is appropriate, as the male ego has had aeons of Apollonian support. His contemporary endorsements include an answering machine and a particularly repellent form of torture used in the prisons of Iran. In some manifestations Apollo would not have shied away from the vast statue that Hitler had planned for him in Berlin. And yet, everywhere, his image is at the apex of the pediment of our palaces of art.

Four

It was in Delphi, so powerfully presided over by Apollo, that *The Trackers of Oxyrhynchus* had its unique one-performance world première on 12 July 1988 in the ancient stadium. It was a joint production between the National Theatre Studio and the European Cultural Centre of Delphi. I have always wanted to prepare a piece for *one* performance. This was what the ancient dramatists did. In the theatre I most admire, poets, and I stress poets, wrote for actors they knew and for a space they knew.

From the beginning, this text was created for two actors, both Yorkshiremen, who had worked with me before in *The Oresteia* and *The Mysteries*. I created the part of Grenfell/Apollo for Jack Shepherd and the part of Hunt/Silenus for Barrie Rutter. It is more than half the battle of creation to know the instruments you are writing for. The space, too, was important. The International Meeting of Ancient Drama which takes place in Delphi every year was inspired by the first festival at Delphi set up by the Greek poet Angelos Sikelianos and his American wife, Eva Palmer, in 1927. For their dramatic performances they used the ancient theatre, lower down the slope and closer to the Temple of Apollo. Nowadays the ancient stadium is used, but with a wooden platform at one end of the racetrack, as if that differently structured curve at one end were the seating of an ancient theatrical space. I resolved to dispense with the platform and use the entire stadium space. This helped to dramatize a contemporary division in our culture between sport and art. In the Pythian Games with its athletics and flute contests, poetry and drama, held on this site, such a division would have been incomprehensible. As would the division between tragedy and satyr play, 'high' art and 'low' art. And in honour of that ancient wholeness we performed our piece, and we became *Ichneutae*, 'Trackers', seeking in fragments of our past and present a common wholeness, a common illumination, a common commitment to survival.

Five

Our 'technical' rehearsals lasted throughout the night of the 11th until after dawn on the 12th. The night had had unusual wild weather and the rocks of the Phaedriades surrounding the stadium concentrated and confined the winds there. The expedition tent of Grenfell and Hunt was blown away. Our papyrus flapped and struggled to be free and fly off to join the eagles that hung over Delphi. We never finished our rehearsal. I had to cover the possibility that the same thing might happen on the 12th. The relay race I had planned, to define the space of the stadium and give us ghosts of its ancient function to awaken the roars of the thousands who once sat at the Pythian Games, had unfortunately dwindled down to one solitary runner who ran like an ancient Marathon runner bearing an Olympic, or should we say Pythian, torch.

Three hours before our première I wrote and gave the following lines to Barrie Rutter to cover both for the expectation of new destructive gusts and to accommodate the solitary, message-bearing runner:

> Everything we've searched for, everything we found
> goes in Grenfell's mania, round and round.
> Grenfell's recurrent nightmare recreates
> careering caravans of Oxyrhynchus crates,
> crates of papyri in a never ending train
> and fragments like a hurricane hurtling through his brain
> and voices, thousands, from the ancient past
> exhorting him to find the 'Ichneftes' FAST!
> That's Grenfell's nightmare and I could add
> another like it that could make everybody mad.
> That the play in the papyrus should reach the light
> in the Stadium of Delphi on a very windy night.
> Last night the wind blew and it stripped
> the stage of everything but actors and a script.
> Let's concentrate, and despite the gusty weather,
> reconstruct the 'Ichneftes' μαζι 'together'.
> Memory runs a marathon, a human mind relay
> from century to century to recreate our play.
> Memory, mother of the Muses, frees
> from oblivion the 'Ichneftes' of Sophocles.

T. H., Newcastle-upon-Tyne, 1989

CHARACTERS

BERNARD PYNE GRENFELL/APOLLO
ARTHUR SURRIDGE HUNT/SILENUS
KYLLENE
HERMES
CHORUS OF FELLAHEEN/SATYRS/FOOTBALL
HOOLIGANS

This play was first performed in the Ancient Stadium of Delphi, Greece, on 12 July 1988, with the following company:

GRENFELL/APOLLO	Jack Shepherd
HUNT/SILENUS	Barrie Rutter
KYLLENE	Juliet Stevenson
HERMES	Dave Hill
	Peter Andrew
CHORUS OF FELLAHEEN/SATYRS/	Christopher Beck
FOOTBALL HOOLIGANS	Stephen Bent
	Jim Bywater
	Lawrence Evans
	Billy Fellows
	Dave Hill
	John O'Hara
	Philip Middlemiss
	Stephen Petcher
	Simon Rackham
	Clive Rowe
Director	Tony Harrison
Design and Lighting	Jocelyn Herbert
Composer	Stephen Edwards
Music Director	Dave Osbon
Company Stage Manager	Trish Montemuro
Stage Manager	Chantal Hauser
Sound	John Rule
Assistant Lighting Designer	Paul McLeish
Scene Painters and Lighting	Chris Bowlby
Operators	Luke Hallam
	Jane Harrison
	Max Harrison
Dance Arranger	Lawrence Evans
Assistant to the Designer	Vicki Hallam
Design Apprentice	Tim Hatley

2

ACKNOWLEDGEMENTS

Grateful thanks for support and assistance in bringing
The Trackers of Oxyrhynchus to the Ancient Stadium of Delphi
are due to:

    The John S. Cohen Foundation

    The Leventis Foundation

    Dr Marianne McDonald

Oliver Taplin and François Lissarague were also most generous
with enthusiasm and inside knowledge of satyrdom.

Photographs pp. 5–8 by Vicki Hallam, pp. 96–8 by Sandra
Lousada.

Tony Harrison and Jocelyn Herbert,
Ancient Stadium of Delphi, May 1988

Dangerous winds blowing the papyrus, technical rehearsal day

5

Kyllene (Juliet Stevenson) on the stage supported by Satyrs
(Billy Fellows, Stephen Bent, Philip Middlemiss)

6

Rehearsals in the Ancient Stadium of Delphi with backdrops
of papyri and behind them the Phaedriades

Silenus (Barrie Rutter)

8

BERNARD PYNE GRENFELL *(1869–1926) and* ARTHUR SURRIDGE HUNT *(1871–1934), the Holmes and Watson of British papyrology, are in the typical gear of Englishmen in the desert, baggy khaki shorts, solar topis. There is a tent and outside it a table made from expedition crates at which* HUNT *sits, logging the finds of the papyri rolls that* GRENFELL *hands him. They are both supervising a* CHORUS OF FELLAHEEN *who from a mound of sand are extracting rolls of papyrus which are passed along the chain of twelve, thrown, juggled, until they finally reach* GRENFELL *who scrutinizes them and rapidly interprets their contents. There are smaller mounds of sand between the main one and the expedition tent. They represent the rubbish mounds of the ancient Egyptian town of Oxyrhynchus. There are numerous expedition crates scattered around waiting to be filled with accumulated papyri and eventually carted away on simple, rough carts. The crates are marked 'Egypt Exploration Fund'.*

As the CHORUS OF FELLAHEEN *scrabble for, extract, produce, throw, and juggle the papyri, they make a chant formed from the lost plays of Sophocles, with the refrain:* Ichneutae *(Ixneytéς)* Ichneutae *(Ixneytéς)* Ichneutae *(Ixneytéς).*

GRENFELL
We're trackers (Ιχνευτες) and what we seek
are fragments of papyri in ancient Greek.
We've filled a few crates full already this week.
Here are treasures crated, waiting to be shipped
from Egypt back to Oxford where we work out each script.
First we dig, then we decipher, then we must
deduce all the letters that have mouldered into dust.

Here at Oxyrhynchus where there's never been much rain
are rubbish heaps of riches. All these mounds contain
preserved papyri from the distant past.
These mounds need excavating fast . . . fast . . . fast.

9

Rubbish heaps of riches! Quite a paradox
there are priceless papyri in every crate and box,
from mundane wage bills for labour on a road
to fragments of a long-lost Sapphic Ode.
These chaps, our fellaheen, can't see what's unique
about scraps of old papyrus in ancient Greek.
We ship back papyri to decipher them at Queen's
but they'd use them, if we let them, as compost for their green
Bits of Sappho, Sophocles and Plato
used as compost for the carrot and potato!

Papyri! Insects gnaw them. Time corrodes
and native plants get potted in a mulch of Pindar's Odes!
Horrible to contemplate! How can a person sleep
while Sophocles is rotting on an ancient rubbish heap?
Our fellaheen, though, are not entirely sure
if Menander's not more use to them as manure!
They ferret for fertilizer, and Hunt and I track
for philosophy and drama in nitrogenous *sebakh*.
Spinach now flourishes from the pulped-up roll
that held still hidden secrets of Sappho's soul.

Flinders Petrie's finds were the inspiration
that put us on the track of this present excavation.
(A hundred years ago exactly. The date
was July 1888.)
Petrie dug Hawara, and discovered there
a papyrus of Homer with a lock of lady's hair.
A hundred years ago almost to the day
I gazed on that Homer in a Bodleian display.
I swore, while still a teenager at Queen's,
to rescue Greek papyri from enriching Egypt's greens.
I was restless, restless. I could scarcely ever rest.
I became, I suppose, quite utterly obsessed.
I lay awake thinking how one day I too might
bring forgotten masterworks back to the light.

The first thing that I did was get a job
with Petrie excavating Coptos and Gurob.
Then after a tedious bureaucratic battle
I excavated Kum-Aushim and Umam-el-Atl.
By December I was able to bring Hunt out here
and '95 began our joint papyri-ing career.

(HUNT *comes out of tent*)

Here at Oxyrhynchus our excavations
lived up to, and surpassed, all expectations.
Crate after crate shipped off, load after load
from laundry list and ledgerwork to tragedy and ode.

(FELLAHEEN *activity increases. Exit* GRENFELL *into tent.*)

HUNT

We have *both* become obsessive. So many loads per hour
or they end up as compost on some Cairo cauliflower.
If one of our backs were turned our fellaheen
would be sloshing Bacchylides on their aubergine.
If we're not double-quick the local folk
will mix Homer and camel dung to grow their artichoke.
Find any fragment however frail or teeny
before it goes to fertilize fellaheen *zucchini*.
I suppose that a compost of ancient Greeks
as good a way as any to grow successful leeks.
We had to be a bit manic not to slip behind,
one digging and deciphering, one logging each new find.

(GRENFELL *comes out of tent and goes back in.*)

Grenfell gets so anxious to recover even scraps
it's brought the poor chap almost close to a collapse.
Grenfell's fast at everything he does. He can *read*
what most people can't decipher at double speed.
Grenfell's electrical, so mercurial and quick
I often fear the work will make my old friend sick.

Grenfell's torrential, so dazzlingly fast
I sometimes fear his sanity might not last.
I worry about Grenfell. Only last year
he said the god Apollo was shouting in his ear.
Apollo pursuing him. Grenfell couldn't rest
till he became, I have to say, almost literally possessed.
He viewed the way our names were in conjuction –
Grenfell–Hunt as an Apollonian injunction.
He heard Apollo yammering for scraps and tatters
of some lost Sophoclean play called *The Tracking Satyrs*.
'Grenfell, Hunt!' he heard the voice abjure,
'Prevent Apollo's favourite play becoming mere manure.
Grenfell! Hunt!' The god's voice went on speaking
putting Grenfell in a panic of papyri-seeking.
Night and day the voice went. 'Grenfell, Bernard Pyne,
hunt for my papyrus. This order is divine!'

(FELLAHEEN *activity intensified. They extract, throw, juggle,
pass on the flying papyri, which* GRENFELL *opens, deciphers
and passes to the seated* HUNT *to log. Their chant goes under
and between the* GRENFELL/HUNT *exchanges.*)

GRENFELL
(*Deciphering papyri*)

> Petition concerning repayment of loan . . .
> Petition complaining of . . . moan . . . moan . . .
>   moan . . .

(*He passes papyrus impatiently to* HUNT *who logs and completes
the find.*)

HUNT
(*Half speed, writing down* GRENFELL'*s deciphering.*)

> Petition concerning repayment of loan
> Petition complaining of . . . non-payment of loan.

12

GRENFELL

Letter on beer tax to the ταραχευται 'mummifiers'.

HUNT

But ταραχευται might mean 'salt-fish suppliers'.

GRENFELL

It might! It might! It might! It might! It might!
God! I do wish some *literature* would come to light.

Petition, petition, receipt, receipt, receipt.
Orders for the payment of supplies of wheat.

HUNT

(*Half speed, writing*)

Petition, petition, receipt, receipt, receipt.
Orders for the payment of supplies of wheat.

GRENFELL

Petitions, petitions, receipts and leases . . .

HUNT

(*Half speed, writing*)

Petitions, petitions, receipts and leases . . .
Can't call these finds lost masterpieces.

KYLLENE

(*From inside tent*)

φοβος εχει με των τοτε κακων
η Δημνια χθων Υψιπυλην . . . woe, O woe

GRENFELL

Not now! Not now! We'll let you know!

(*To* HUNT)
Did you hear that, that tragic moan?

HUNT
Take a rest, Bernard. I can manage alone.

GRENFELL
(*Back to deciphering*)

Acknowledgement of loan of vegetable seed
and . . . and . . . and . . . the rest I can't read.

(*He hands papyrus to* HUNT.)

HUNT
(*Studies and completes.*)

Sale of donkey . . . 56 Drachs!

GRENFELL
Receipt for payment of cattle tax . . .

Petition, petition, Ptolemaic 2 AD . . .
and . . . and . . . and . . . now let me see! –
letter from Gemellius . . . (in terrible condition!)
Seems to be some sort of

(*He hands papyrus to* HUNT.)

HUNT
Petition!

GRENFELL
Fragments of accounts concerning wheat . . .
Arthur, the date . . . I admit defeat.

(*He hands papyrus to* HUNT.)

See if you can do better than me.

                    HUNT
2nd BC!

                    KYLLENE
(*From inside tent*)

        ως απολλυμαι κακως
        οι φοβοι δ, εχουσι με, O woe! O woe!

                    GRENFELL
(*To* HUNT)

        Did you hear that, like a woman's death-throes,
        a cry from far away, so full of fear?

                    HUNT
(*Alarmed and concerned*)

        I think you need rest. Go inside for a doze.
        Don't want you laid up. I'll manage things here.
        Don't want you laid up like you were last year.

                    GRENFELL
(*Ignoring* HUNT *and even more frantically passing on rolls*)

        Census!

                    HUNT
Census!

                    GRENFELL
Petition, report, report, report.

                    HUNT
Petition, report, report, report.

GRENFELL

Judicial proceedings, minutes of the court.

HUNT

(*Half speed, writing*)

Judicial proceedings, minutes of the court.

GRENFELL

O, what's that! Something that I almost missed,
the verso of that Oxyrhynchus census list . . .

(*Pause to decipher.*)

O, it's . . . Pindar . . . Pindar . . . but not all there!
A paean for the people of . . . of . . . but where?
A paean by Pindar hitherto unknown . . .

(HUNT *rises from his table and they both scan the papyrus.*)

GRENFELL *and* HUNT

(*In almost childish wonder*)

A paean of Pindar hitherto unknown . . .

(*Reading the Greek together*)

Κασταλιας . . . . . Απολλωνος . . . . . θαμινα Δελφων!

A paean of Pindar hitherto unknown . . .
for the people of Delphi,
                    lost till this minute.

HUNT

Castalia

GRENFELL

(*Transfixed, listening for the god in his ear*)

Apollo!

Delphi! They're all in it!

(*The* CHORUS OF FELLAHEEN *switch from their 'searching chant' which has been present under the above and begin to chant to the audience in the stadium of Delphi Pindar's newly discovered 'Paean for the People of Delphi'.**)

Προς Ολυμπιου Διος σε, Χρυσεα
κλυτομαντι Πυθοι,
Λισσομαι Χαριτεσ –
σιν τε και συν Αφροδιτα,
εν ζαθεω με δεξαι χρονω
αοιδιμων Πιεριδων προφαταν.
υδατι γαρ επι Χαλκοπυλω
ψοφον αιων Κασταλιας
ορφανον ανδρων χορευσιος ηλθον
εταις αμαχανιαν αλεξων
τεοισιν εμαις τε τιμαις.
ητορι δε φιλω παις ατε μητερι κεδνα
πειθομενος κατεβαν στεφανων
και θαλιαν τροφον αλσος Α –
πολλωνος τοθι, Λατοιδαν
θαμινα Δελφων κοραι χθονος ομφαλον
παρα σκιαεντα μελπομεναι
ποδι κροτεοντι γαν θοω.

(*The* CHORUS OF FELLAHEEN *complete their performance of the 'Paean for the People of Delphi', then fall to searching in the mounds of sand again. In the silence that follows we hear the* VOICE OF APOLLO *from the rear screen where his image from the Delphi plate is projected. The* VOICE OF APOLLO *is speaking the first fragmentary lines of the* Ichneutae *of Sophocles as if from the distant past.* GRENFELL, *who has been frozen in rapt attention since he discovered the word 'Apollo' in the Paean,*

*For music to 'Pindar's Hymn' see p.74

and heard it chanted by the FELLAHEEN, *is being taken over by* APOLLO. *He is partially on the way to 'becoming'* APOLLO.)

VOICE OF APOLLO

. . .]σ[. . .
. . . .]κιο[. . .
. . . .]πειτα[. . .
. . . .]πεσσυϑ[. . .
. . . . . .]γ[. . . . .]λ[. . .
. . . .]ω[. . .

(*then* GRENFELL *speaks to himself as* APOLLO *and begins a frantic dialogue with his 'alter ego'.*)

GRENFELL
Apollo

That Paean was fine and full of my praises
but I want that play where I speak the phrases.

Grenfell

But I'm working as fast as I possibly can.

Apollo

I suppose that you are being only a man.

Grenfell

Please leave me alone. Please, please go away.

Apollo

I'll pursue you until you track down my play.

Grenfell

I promise. I promise. New get out of my mind.

Apollo

No, till you find it I'll stay right behind.

Grenfell

I have a pistol, Apollo. I might have to shoot.

Apollo

And you might just regret that, Grenfell, old fruit.
Find the papyrus and fill in the gaps!

Grenfell

I'm working too hard. I'm damned near to collapse.

18

Do you realize how much time we require?
> *Apollo*

Do *you* realize I require my *lyre*?
Remember Cassandra. I brought her to heel.
> *Grenfell*

I wouldn't have thought that I had her appeal.
> *Apollo*

Don't be too sure! Just keep on the track
and remember Apollo's right at your back.
Somewhere there's a play where I come on first.
> *Grenfell*

Stop it! Stop it! My brain's going to burst.
Such literary finds are exceedingly few
> *Apollo*

Bernard, old boy, I'm counting on you.

> *Grenfell*

(*Producing papyrus*)

I've found this one. Will this one do?
> *Apollo*

If I get a part or a mention or two.
> *Grenfell*

It's a poem praising Theon from 3 A D .
> *Apollo*

Praising Theon! What about me?
> *Grenfell*

Where may I ask did you study your Greek?
> *Apollo*

What's dead to you, dear, I actually speak.
I know Greek a damn sight better than you.
επτατονον χειρεσσι . . . shall I construe?

(*Reads Greek rapidly:*)

επτατονον χειρεσσι λυρην πολυηχεα κρουων
την αυτος τα πρωτα καμες παρα ποσσι τεκουοης
'The lyre in exchange for the bulls of Apollo' . . .
The rest's difficult Greek that you might not follow.

Grenfell
Almost an alpha I think that you pass.
Apollo
You'll get gamma minus rammed up your arse.
But you know very well that this fragment won't do
There's not enough of it, I'm mute, and the you
isn't me that the poem's lines address
I want my play, my play, the *Ichneftés*
alas, long ago vanished into nothingness.

(*Begins the fragments again.*)
        απαντα χρηοτα . . .
                        Grenfell
                        Go to hell!
                HUNT
(*Looking up from his engrossing logging*)

Bernard, are you all right? Are you feeling unwell?

                GRENFELL
I'm fine! I'm fine! I'm fine! I'm fine! I'm fine!
                Apollo
(*Mimicking*)

Bernard! You'd better discover that play of mine.

(*APOLLO now taunts GRENFELL with more fragments of the lost play.*)

        ]αξ[. . . . . .]λιθι[. . . . . .]στρ[. . . . . .]μηπ[. . .
                        Grenfell
Leave me alone. You must let me sleep.
                        Apollo
. . .]αρου[. . . . . .]ουα[. . . . . .]ρια[. . .
                        Grenfell
Go away! Leave me! Get away from here.
                        Apollo
. . .]λει[. . . . . .]γ[. . . . . .]φλεβο[. . . . . .]μη[

                        20

Grenfell

Lost. Lost. In the limbo of history.

Apollo

. . .]ατημε[. . . . .]ονιου β[. . . . . .]μη φυ[. . .

Grenfell

I'm doing the utmost a mere mortal can do.

Apollo

απαντα χρηστα και . . . . . . something . . . . . . λειν

Grenfell

Stop it! I can't get that phrase from my brain.

Apollo

απαντα χρηστα και . . . . . . something . . . . . . λειν

Grenfell

Stop it! Stop it! You'll drive me insane.

Apollo

απαντα χρηστα και . . . . . . something . . . . . . λειν

Grenfell

I beg of you, *please*. Don't say that again.

Apollo

(Changing the taunting fragment momentarily)

. . .]σ[. . .] κιο [. . . . . .] πειτα [. . .]πεσσυϑ[. . .
]γ[. . .]λ[. . . . . .]ω[. . .

What goes in the gaps, Grenfell? Come on, you know.

Grenfell

I don't! I don't. Go! Go! Go!

Apollo

απαντα χρηστα και . . . . . . something . . . λειν

You've got to use that mercurial brain
and put all my missing letters in,
from this instant I'm in you and using your skin.
Find me the play where these fragments go

. . .]σ[. . .]κιο[. . . . . .]πειτα[. . . . . .]πεσσυϑ[
. . .]γ[. . .]λ[. . . . . .]ω[. . . *etc. etc.*

(*This fragment is now again in the air from the rear screen and*
GRENFELL *rushes round the expedition tent 'pursued' by*
APOLLO.

21

*Finally, in panic and exasperation he fires his pistol at the
imagined phantom of* APOLLO. *This shot sets off a relay race
between the* FELLAHEEN *in three teams of four, with papyrus
rolls as batons. The 'relay race' (which also represents the race
against time of Grenfell's and Hunt's papyrology) is run along
the laid out tracks in the stadium from the front screen to the rear
screen. We hear during the race, as the 'music', the sound of
some 8000 ghosts 2000 years ago, say, in Pindar's time. The
chants of these ancient spectators are based on fragments of the*
Ichneutae. *These fragments we will, later, associate with the*
CHORUS OF SATYRS. *The winning papyrus/baton is
presented to* HUNT.)

VOICE OF APOLLO

. . .]σ[. . .
. . . . . .]κιο[. . .
. . . .]πειτα[. . .
. . . . . .]πεσσυϑ[. . .
. . . .]γ[. . .]λ[. . .]ω[. . .

(*Immediately we hear from the rear screen the 'Apollo'
fragments which have the immediate effect of changing*
GRENFELL *into* APOLLO, *or at least effecting the first stage of
his transformation.* HUNT *goes into the expedition tent.*)

GRENFELL/APOLLO
(*Emerging from rubbish tip spitting out* APOLLO*'s fragments*)

. . .]σ[. . .
. . . . . .]κιο[. . .
. . . .]πειτα[. . .
. . . . . .]πεσσυϑ[. . .
. . . .]γ[. . .]λ[. . .]ω[. . .

I'm a god, Apollo, but I was tipped
on a rubbish heap inside this manuscript.
I've spent centuries asleep
on an Oxyrhynchus rubbish heap.

You can imagine my fine Olympian feelings
tossed on to a tip with old potato peelings.
Till 1907 I had to wait
when Grenfell and Hunt came to excavate.
Covered in rubbish! But what's much worse is
being resurrected with only half my verses.
Converted into dust and bookworm excreta,
riddled lines with just the ghost of their metre.
All my speeches, all my precious words
mounting mounds of dust and millipede turds.
Ages under rubbish, sand and desert heat
and then be resurrected only half complete.
One used to the heights of Mount Parnassos
buried under dirt and drab domestic dross.
That's bad enough. But fate's not really fair
to have me only half restored, and not all there!
It's pathetic! Half the things I say
time or the desert mites have gnawed away.

Enough complaining though. Now no more ado –
straight into the script and go right through.
And bit by bit we'll try to pick our way
slowly back through time and this lost satyr play.

Though I'm a deity and in everything divine
I still can get kerpertled about my kine.
You can't imagine how much it deeply grieves
even a god like me to lose his beeves.
My heart, though an immortal's, absolutely breaks
to think of all my loved ones turned into steaks.
It drives me out of my Apollonian mind
tracking down those cattle I just can't find.

Some light-fingered lout has filched my kine
that now could be kebabs washed down with wine.
Some villain, some unscrupulous thief's
probably turned my cows into ροσβιφ [*rosbif*]
I want them back at once or even sooner

before they're barbecued στα καρβομνα [*sta karvouna*]
Some dissembling cattle-rustling shit
's got them, at this minute, browning on his spit.
Even for a god the way's hard-going
ears pricked for the slightest sound of lowing.

(*Listens*)

Listen! Nothing! Listen! . . . Oh I knew
each of my darlings by her distinctive moo.

(*Calls Greek names*:)

Κανελλω μου . . . Ασπρουλα μου . . . Παρδαλω μου . . .
Λενιω μου . . . Αρχοντα μου . . . Μαρυουλα μου . . .
Αστηρης μου . . .

Listen! Nothing! Some despicable slob
has done a stealthy cattle-rustling job.
I've been all over Greece. So far. So far!
I bet my bulls are in some bugger's abattoir.
I've been so far, following their trail
the length and breadth of Greece to no avail.
Who'd commit the sacrilege? Who could steal
my little loved ones and convert them into veal?
For a moment I thought I could discern a
somewhat suspicious sniff from a taverna.
It seemed to me that smell might mean a
meal of my moo-cows swilled down with retsina.

I'm almost out of my godlike mind
tracking those nicked cows I just can't find.
Who'd commit the sacrilege? Who'd dare? Who'd dare
to spirit off my herd into the air?
Man or immortal? It's hard to believe
someone could have had the cheek to thieve
the cattle of the Sungod out of their byre.
I'm as furious as the Furies in the *Oresteia*.

24

Thessaly, Boeotia, the Doric (space . . . space . . .
space)
then quickly to Kyllene, that's this place.
So, shepherd, farmer, charcoal burner,
layabout in the taverna,
and, maybe in rustic parts like these,
descended from the dryades,
the children of wild woodland creatures
with half human and half goat/horse features,
if *any* find my cattle stolen from their lord,
Apollo, and returns them, he'll get a good reward.
There's bakhsheesh for the body who can track
down my stolen herd and bring them back.

HUNT

(*From inside tent*)

Grenfell, Bernard, are you sure you're all right?
Shall I come out and give you a hand?
Enough work for today. You'll ruin your sight.
It's too dark to decipher or dig in the sand.

APOLLO

Hunt!

HUNT

(*From inside tent*)

Just a minute, just getting dressed.

APOLLO

Hunt out more fragments and find me the rest.
Hunt!

HUNT

(*From inside tent*)

Coming!

25

Hunt for my kine.

(*From the expedition tent enter* HUNT *now as* PAPPA
SILENUS, *the leader of the* CHORUS OF SATYRS)

SILENUS
Ιασου, Apollo, care for some wine?

I heard your proclamation, sir, and ran
or came as quickly as an old geezer can.
Us satyrs can help you. Our horse-like sniffers
will soon track down your heisted bulls and heifers,
and, maybe, win, divine Apollo, Lord,
whatever you're offering by way of reward.
If you could see your way, your honour, to bestowing
bakhsheesh on the boys, I'll get them going.
Summat beneficial. They'd have no quarrel
with gold or food, or liquid from a barrel,
but don't reckon too much to a wreath of laurel.
Summat solid, Lord Apollo, please,
not leaf equivalents of OBEs.
A bit of wilting boskage for the brows
falls far short of casks for a carouse.
Or cash to buy the casks if the supply
of buckshee Dionysian has all run dry.
A nightmare too monstrous to take in
A thirst like mine and no wine in this skin –
The prospect of promotion to Sir Satyr
doesn't make my heart go pitter-patter.
You know us, all prancing, getting pissed
so forget your Olympian Honours List.
Summat solid. Are we both agreed?
If so, I'll get the lads out at top speed.

APOLLO
I must say I find you commendably keen.
I'll make you the foreman of my fellaheen.

I'll put you in charge of my trackers, I mean.

SILENUS
My boys'll do their bit. Your bulls'll get tracked
but the reward, remember. Don't forget our pact.
And now to the task in hand. Now, rightaway
I'll bring my loyal lads into the play.

(SILENUS *gazes towards the rear screen where the shadow
puppets of* SATYRS *are projected.* APOLLO *looks at them.*
APOLLO *stays gazing at the shadows which begin to move.*
SILENUS *turns towards the audience and takes out a referee's
whistle.*)

I'll whistle up those loyal lads of mine.

(SILENUS *blows the referee's whistle. The* SATYRS *move. But
do not enter. Blows again.* APOLLO *moves closer to rear screen.
Nothing.*)

APOLLO
(*Shouting back to* SILENUS)

You've lost your herd like me. I see no sign.

SILENUS
I assure you, sir, that's not the case. Oh no
my lads are like lightning just as I am slow.
All Pappa Silenus has to do is click
his fingers and they'll be here in just one tick.

(SILENUS *clicks his fingers.* APOLLO *stares. The shadows
move. But the* SATYRS *do not enter.*)

If I take my middle finger and my thumb
and click them together. They'll come. *They'll come!*

(SILENUS *clicks confidently.* APOLLO *stares at shadows. Nothing.*)

APOLLO

(*Moving even further up towards rear screen*)

> Well? Well? Where are they? Nothing to be seen.
> They're unreliable like the fellaheen.

SILENUS

> There's only one thing left to try
> a few new-found fragments from the *Ichneutae*.
>
> Sorry, Erasmian! What I'm saying is if we shout
> some fragments of *Ichneftés* my satyrs will come out.

(SILENUS *takes a papyrus scroll and unrolls it to reveal some fragments of the Greek papyrus, in fact, the first words of the Chorus of Satyrs in their fragmentary, incomplete state. They should be legible to all. With this he begins to teach the audience to chant the fragments until there is a strong chant which is echoed by the ancient voices of the 8000 ghosts at the ancient Pythian Games.*)

> ιϑ αγε δ [. . . . . .]
> ποδα βα [. . . . . .]
> απαπαπ [. . . . . .]
> ω ω σε τοι [. . . . . .]

(*To* APOLLO *waiting for the Satyrs*)

> Are they coming out? Are all my satyrs here?

APOLLO

> No, they're stuck in the papyrus and don't want to
>   appear.

(SILENUS *once more gets the audience to chant the fragments*

and once more the shadows move and the chant from the living
audience is taken up by the 8000 ghosts of the Pythian Games.)

SILENUS

ιϑ αγε δ] . . . . . . [
ποδα βα] . . . . . . [
απαπαπ] . . . . . . [
ω ω σε τοι] . . . . . . [

Haven't they appeared, your great Apolloship?

APOLLO
Not the faintest sign of a satyr phallus tip!

SILENUS
Just one more chorus of ιϑ αγε δ . . .

APOLLO
It's hopeless, like trying to bring back the dead.
But, if you must, one more chorus. Go ahead.
If you have any luck once you've got your lads out
I'll be down in my temple. Give me a shout.

(*Exit* APOLLO *towards the Temple of Apollo*.)

SILENUS

ιϑ αγε δ] . . . . . . [
ποδα βα] . . . . . . [
απαπαπ] . . . . . . [
ω ω σε τοι] . . . . . . [

(*The chant is repeated by the audience and echoed by the 8000*
ghosts of the ancient Pythian Games who are watching an athletic
contest. APOLLO *is almost up to the rear screen waiting for the*
shadow puppets to emerge from the screen.

SILENUS *cuts off the audience's chant, and in the ensuing*
silence suddenly the twelve crates stencilled 'Egypt Exploration

29

Fund' fall open together revealing in each a SATYR *and so
forming a* CHORUS OF TWELVE SATYRS. *The twelve crates
open forwards, backwards and sideways and create a
labyrinthine platform of crosses on which are painted the tracks
of Apollo's herd. This maze platform is where the* SATYRS
*perform their dance. They wear clogs. These 'hoofs' make them
the original 'hoofers'.*

They pick up the chant of Greek fragments that SILENUS,
*the audience and the 8000 ghosts of the Pythian Games had
summoned them up with.*)

(*To audience and ghosts*)

> Ευχαριστω, you living. Ευχαριστω, you dead,
> you've brought my boys back with your ιϑ αγε δ.

(*To* SATYRS)

> After two thousand years, lads, look, there's your text.
> It's up to you, to track what comes next.
> And once you've tracked down each missing Greek
>   word
> then sniff out the trail of Apollo's lost herd.

CHORUS OF SATYRS*
Group B
ιϑ αγε δ . . . . . . (bracket . . . bracket . . .)
Group C
ποδα βα . . . . . . (bracket . . . bracket . . .)
Group A
απαπαπ . . . . . . (bracket . . . bracket . . .)
Group B
ω ω σε τοι . . . . . . (bracket . . . bracket . . .)
Where cows tread . . . (track it . . . track it . . .)

---

*For music to 'Tracking Satyrs' Dance' see p.82

30

near or far . . . (track it . . . track it . . .)
Group A
seek cow-clap . . . (track it . . . track it . . .)
Group B
however wee . . . (track it . . . track it . . .)
επιϑι κλωπ . . . . . . (βραψκετ . . .)
Group C
υπονομα κ . . . . . . (bracket . . .)
Group A
Don't give up hope . . . (track it . . .)
Group B
We'll get them back . . . (track it . . .)

(*The* CHORUS OF TWELVE SATYRS *now begin to follow the marked maze-like tracks and become a parody of the Furies in the National Theatre* Oresteia, *sniffing for the blood of Orestes. At first their respective tracks avoid one another, but only just.*)

Group B

Sniff, sniff
sniff at the track
we've gotta get t' god's cattle back.

Group C

Sniff, sniff
sniff at the dung
t'devil who did this is gonna get 'ung.

Group A

Sniff, sniff
sniff every turd
t'droppings'll lead us t'god's 'erd.

Group B

Sniff, sniff
sniff left and right
sniff every tincture of cattle shite.

31

Group C

Sniff, sniff
sniff every clue
sniff every sort of numero two.

Group A

Sniff, sniff
sniff without stopping
sniff every turd, sniff every dropping.

Group B

Sniff, sniff
sniff t'shit on t'ground
t'cattle-rustler's gotta be found.

(*The* SATYRS' *maze/tracking dance continues and becomes
faster as though they are getting closer to their prey, then,
following their different tracks they end in collision. They fall
down, then they begin to look at the tracks closely*.)

1

If these are bull's tracks, their back legs go first.
These bulls have had their bums reversed.

2

These tracks of god's herd, if that's what we've found
Look they're all of 'em the wrong way round.

3

Hey, look here at this! It's stupid, daft.
Their backlegs are forrad, their front legs aft.

4

Blow me some bugger's done a switch.
Head or arsehole, which is which?

5

Eeh bah gum, and ecky thump

this un's face must be in its rump.

6

Some force has sent us out of our minds
Cows don't moo from their behinds.

(*The* SATYRS *begin to track again. They reprise their chant,
and again end up colliding.*

*Suddenly there is an eerie sound which stops them dead in their
tracks. (This eerie sound is the sound of the newly invented lyre,
the first stringed instrument.) The* SATYRS' *clogs start
chattering with fear on the crate platform.*)

1

That sound!

2

'orrible!

3

Frightening!

4

Scary!

5

Spooky!

ALL

(*To audience*)
It's the prototype of the bazouki!

6

Don't care what it is. I'm off back in
that papyrus! Stuff all this tracking!

33

You're pathetic. You're all made of jelly.
Every man-beast of you's a yeller belly.
You cowardly creeps, you dastardly dogs
you're not fit to buckle or bull up my clogs.
The buzz of a few lobelia-browsing bees
has you lot trembling at the knees.
Some shepherd's yell, some midget poodle's yap
and your clogs are all clarted with panicker's crap.
Unmanned, un*horsed* by some moggy's meak miaou
made into cowards by one moo from a cow.

And if that sound had the merest hint of moo
it might be the herd these tracks have led to.
Scared of your own shadow, no spunk, no spine
all talk and tupping, no true sons of mine.
Bragging and shagging, that's your style
but show you real action and you run a mile.
You say you'll stick by me, but come the crunch
you turn out such a yeller-bellied bunch.

But Silenus in his day, he never fled.
He faced all dangers with no shred of dread.
Silenus the Satyr, never short of spunk,
braved every battle, never did a bunk.
He was a warrior, valorous, not weak,
not thrown in a panic by a mere squawk or squeak.
When fierce battle raged I never quit –
there I was always in the thick of it.
A hero with honour from many a campaign,
an honour your cowardice will now stain.
Think of an old soldier having to see
his own battalion turn tail and flee.
The ones he brags about as his 'brave boys'
ready to desert the field because of a mere noise,
some squawk, some squeak, some tu-whit-tu-whoo.
A fieldmouse's fart's enough to scare you.
Fabled as I am for many a noble feat

it breaks this soldier's heart to see you in retreat.

You'd piss off if you heard a parrot sneeze.

CHORUS OF SATYRS
1
Come here then, you hero, and play Hercules.

2
Yer, come here yourself, if you have no fear.

3
If you are so brave, then come over here.

4
It's all right for you. You're not even near.

5
If you brave dangers then brave this one now.

6
Ay, then tell us we're only scared of some cow.

7
Ay, show us this famous courage of yours.

8
And see how your feel when the grim monster roars.

9
You'll find out we're terrified with good cause.

10
It's a sound like nothing on earth before.

11
It strikes terror in us right down to the core.

35

If you know no fear be the first on the track.

SILENUS

I am the hunter and you are the pack
and the hunter, when tracking, leads from the back.
But if an old soldier has to instil
courage in cowards, then instil I will.
I'll lead the rabble, if you so choose
and pump up your courage with hunter's halloos.
When a fierce commander stands at their head
even base cowards forget to feel dread.
When cowards are led by commanders like me
they see my example, stand fast, and don't flee.

(SILENUS *puffs out his chest, stands erect, and begins to march
with as much dignity as he can muster the platform 'maze'. At
certain specified points he executes a hard-clog shuffle intended
to make the* SATYRS *take courage, stand, and then be prepared
to confront the eerie noise.*

One by one they begin to support the 'bravery dance' of
SILENUS. *The dance reaches a crescendo, then is cut off by the
sound of the hidden newly invented lyre.* SILENUS *hears it.*)

I'll let you do the tracking. I'm getting too old.

(*To audience*)

But I'll be back later for my share of the gold.

(*Exit* SILENUS *to a seat in the audience. But the* SATYRS *are
now heartened and determined to find the source of the strange
noise never heard on earth before. They begin a clattering dance
to rouse the nymph* KYLLENE *who is reposing in the expedition
'tent/tiring house'. Each time they reach a crescendo they stop
and then turn towards the tent, but* KYLLENE, *so eager before,
now misses her cue. During this time some* SATYRS *drop from*

*the dance and begin to build 'The Theatre of Dionysos' in front
of the front papyrus screen. They build this rough theatre from
the 'Egypt Exploration Fund' crates; some open on their sides to
allow three* S A T Y R S *to crouch and appear as though they are
supporting the stage like the figures in the Theatre of Dionysos in
Athens. The dance to rouse the nymph* K Y L L E N E *becomes
more urgent and then slower as the* S A T Y R S *get weary until only
one is left to finally rouse her from the tent.* K Y L L E N E *finally
emerges from the tent. She is a Caryatid, like those supporting
the pediment of the Erectheum in Athens. In as dignified way as
possible she places a vast piece of pediment on her head and
walks slowly from the tent to the stage created by the crates,
mounts the steps and enters on the stage through a gap in the
papyrus screen. Spotlight on screen. Behind the screen*
K Y L L E N E *ascends the steps.*)

KYLLENE

ως απολλυμαι κακως . . . O woe! O woe!

(*Enter* K Y L L E N E *through papyrus curtain.*)

(*Looking down from stage*)

I have a feeling I'm in the wrong show!

(*She speaks only 'high' dated Victorian verse of the kind that
Greek tragedy used to be translated in. Three* S A T Y R S *grunt
under the weight of the* σκηνη *[scene].*)

CHORUS OF SATYRS

I

So calm of body, so serene of face,
drapery discreet, and every hair in place.

2

Them girls are straight but we're not straight
but bent and straining underneath the weight.

37

3

Though it's tons of marble that she holds
A caryatid still looks like a centrefold.

4

The Theatre of Dionysos. Have you seen
the poor satyrs there supporting the scene?

5

We're only half human so we can be shown
sweating and straining underneath the stone.

6

Caryatids carry as their name suggests
but no sweat ever trickled down their breasts.

7

Caryatids carry tons of carved stone
but never let out a grunt or a groan.

8

Horse's ears and tails, but we still have souls
and we're always shoved into supporting roles.

9

Caryatids can, but satyrs aren't allowed
to carry tons of marble and still look proud.

10

Caryatids carry the Erectheum high
but their armpits stay unstinking and dry.

(*The haughty* KYLLENE *who has spent these speeches moving
her pediment-loaded head from speaker to speaker, now begins
to speak and breaks her silence to address those who have
disturbed her calm.*)

KYLLENE

Bestial creatures! Wherefore have you brought
to this secluded spot your uproar foul?
What novel sports are these? They are not they
wherewith of old you made your master glad,
who clad in his fawnskin and with thyrsus high
was wont to chant of yore the holy hymns
with, for escort, nymphs and youthful throngs?

SATYR I

(*Under the stage*)

She means Dionysos, pissed, sang us old songs.

KYLLENE

Now I know not what possesseth you
nor what crazed folly spinneth you awry . . .
I heard like hunters' halloos from deep within
a cry when keen trackers close upon their prey
and hap upon the beast deep in its lair.
And then such harsh words as theft and thief
assailed my ears and some god's proclamation.
Your fragments of furore reached me down there
and then an utter cacophony commenced.
I feared that you would do my person harm.

SATYR I

(*Joining in 'tragic' tone*)

Stay thine anger, nymph of the deep zone.
We are no bringers of disruptive strife.
Nay, all that we humbly wish is that you disclose
the meaning of that hidden sound we heard.

KYLLENE

That is a better way to learn what you desire

39

than by alarming here a poor defenceless nymph.
Quarrels are most distressing to my soul.
Now I implore proceed and make your plea.

SATYR 1

Ruler of this region, Kyllene, Queen,
our purpose later will I you explain.
But this voice we heard, what is it, pray?
It frayed our nerves and set our teeth on edge.
Who is it that bringeth the gooselumps on our flesh?
What is it that raiseth the spine hairs on our back?

KYLLENE

I must advise you ere I do commence,
should you disclose what I to you disclose,
there will be severest suffering in store.

SATYR 2
(*Groaning under weight of stage*)

I wish she'd get to t'point. My back's that sore.

KYLLENE

These things are secret, guarded by the gods.
The heavenly ones keep Hera in the dark.

SATYR 3
(*Under stage*)

Zeus, again, I bet, and some new lascivious lark!

KYLLENE

Zeus hither hied where Maia doth abide
and all unbeknowst to Hera, hither hied
and made the fair one his clandestine bride.

SATYR 1
(*Under stage*)

Zeus never could resist a bit on t'side.

In the cave the nymph brought forth a son
the which, because his mother Maia
doth languish in a fever nurse I in these arms.
But the babe doth burgeon greatly day by day.
'Tis a great wonder to me and a fright.
Born six days ago and yet hath boyhood reached.
He blossometh and shooteth up without a pause.
Such is the babe whose nurture I have here.
We conceal him for his mighty father's sake.

SATYR 1

(*Under stage*)

I wish I could escape, that babe sounds queer.

SATYR 2

(*Under stage*)

Gerronwi'it! Mi back's about to break.

KYLLENE

As for the voice which caused you such affright
bursting forth from some unseen source of sound
it came from something turned the wrong way up.
The babe I nurse devised it in a day
from a dead creature, as a source of joy.
He plays his strange device both night and day.

SATYR 3

(*Under stage*)

I hope that's the end. Mi back's giving way.

SATYR 4

Ay, bugger the whatsit, and the miraculous boy

wanking about with the dead creature toy.

SATYR 5
Excuse me, but how can summat dead, like, sing?

SATYR 6
Ay, how come a voice came from a dead thing?

SATYR 7
Dead but vocal! A corpse that can carol.

SATYR 8
Seems somebody's snout's been into the barrel.

SATYR 9
It's a stiff and it warbles. How come?

SATYR 10
Ay, how come?

KYLLENE
Dead it has a voice. Alive it was dumb.

SATYR 11
Give us a clue. Is it bent, fat, short or what?

KYLLENE
'Tis spotted and shaped somewhat like a pot.

SATYR 12
A leopard, of course, or some sort of cat.

KYLLENE
No, sorry. It isn't at all like that.

SATYR 4
Not a crab, not a lobster, not a crustacean?

SATYR 5

Then it's gotta be the bug part of creation.

SATYR 6

A beetle? The Etna horned scarab, mayhap?

SATYR I

(*Under stage*)

Solve her damned riddle and cut all the crap.

(KYLLENE *moves the vast pediment on her head slowly in
answer to the last guess*.)

SATYR 7

Madam, what bit of it makes that horrible din?

SATYR 8

Does that horrible noise come from outside or in?

KYLLENE

From what you might call the creature's crust.

SATYR 2

(*Under stage*)

Solve the bloody riddle. My head's going to bust.

SATYR 9

If we may be so presumptuous as to inquire.

KYLLENE

(*After a long pause during which the pediment-weighted head
moves from one side to the other*.)

The beast's called a tortoise. The invention's the lyre.

(KYLLENE *indicates the lyre with the baby projected on the*

43

front screen. The SATYRS *listen as the lyre sounds again.*)

CHORUS OF SATYRS

1

It could be a goat
to judge from its note

All
BUT!

2

It could be a duck's
the guts that he plucks

All
BUT!

3

It could be a cat
A cat sounds like that

All
BUT!

4

Dog's gut or hound's
could be making these sounds

All
BUT!

I bet it's bullock gut.

Summat's been flayed
for this sweet serenade

5

It's not just the tortoise's hollow shell
there's some other creature in there as well.

44

Summat's been flayed
for this sweet serenade.

6

It isn't just a tortoise, is it, though?
There's some other sound in it. Some sort of low.

All

Summat's been flayed
for this sweet serenade.

7

Yer, some other sound keeps coming through.
It's more than a tortoise. It's got like a *moo*.

All

Summat's been flayed
for this sweet serenade.

And the question is
to this kid that's a whiz
where did you get that gut?

Them leather thongs
he twangs into songs
to comfort, or, maybe, carouse,
we don't have to go through
the whole bloody zoo
they come from Apollo's nicked cows.

(KYLLENE *is tipped off the stage. her pediment falls. Four*
SATYRS *try to lift it. They can't.* KYLLENE *raises it again with
effortless Olympic lift. Exits with as much dignity as possible.*)

KYLLENE
ως απολλυμαι κακως . . . O woe! O woe!
I'm not in the right play. I'd better go.

45

(*Exit tragedy pursued by a* SATYR.)

CHORUS OF SATYRS

1

Well, we've found Apollo's cattle. We'll be freed.
He'll give us some gold to buy all we need.

2

And that *we* need's not some plaything to pluck.
Satyrs need to get drunk and then fuck.

All

APOLLO! APOLLO! APOLLO!

(*Enter* APOLLO *from the rear screen. He is calling mournfully after his cows using their pet Greek names:*)

APOLLO

Κανελλω μου . . . Ασπρουλα μου . . . Παρδαλω μου . . .
Λενιω μου . . . Αρχοντα μου . . . Μαρυουλα μου . . .
Αστηρης μου . . .

Where are my loved ones, give them to me,
then I'll give you the gold and set you all free.

SATYR 1

You have to face up to it, sir, this 'lyre'
's all you've got left of the bulls from your byre.

SATYR 2

The strings of this thing came from your herd's guts
and these were the horns that waved, once, on their
    nuts.

SATYR 3

And look at this, squire, this membrane of hide.
Bet it came off a flayed bullock's backside.

46

SATYR 4

Them lovely moo-cows you mooned over, squire.
All that's left of the lot is this little lad's lyre.

SATYR 5

Sorry to tell you but this little lad
's squeezed all your steers into t'prototype Strad.

SATYR 6

We've tracked them the length and breadth of the land
And now all they're fit for's to play in a band.

SATYR 7

Your cows have been kaputted by this kid.
She says he's called Hermes, this Caryatid.

SATYR 8

She claims he's her charge, claims she's his nurse
and insists on spouting Victorian verse.

SATYR 9

She's called Kyllene, or so she claims
but I think they're both of 'em assumed names.

SATYR 10

This crappy little chappy we apprehended
she claims that he's Zeus-descended.

SATYR 11

You're a god, squire. Is he one or not?
Does he strike you as one of your lot?

SATYR 12

I'll wager my share of the spoil this widdling wain's
not got a drop of god's blood in his veins.

APOLLO

He'll have to be quizzed this whiz-kid you've tracked

47

and you'll be rewarded, as per our pact.
This bovver babe, this bovicidal maniac.
I'll beat him black and blue to get my bulls back.
I'll skin the bugger. I'll do him in.
I'll make a drum from the little sod's skin.

(*Fluctuates between rage and grief and fascination with the
sounds the guts of his pets now send into the air about him.*)

Fetch him out. Fetch him out. He'll feel my fist
this infant . . . instrumentalist . . .

CHORUS OF SATYRS
Fetch him out! Fetch him out! Fetch him out!

(*The* SATYRS *begin a 'Fetch him out!' chant like 'Here we go'
and also stamp a rhythm on the platforms. It reaches a crescendo
and there is a silence and expectation in which* APOLLO *repeats
his threat.*)

APOLLO
Fetch him out. Fetch him out. He'll feel my fist
this infant . . . instrumentalist . . .

(*Enter from the gap in the papyrus a large* HERMES *in a nappy
made of papyrus scraps. He terrifies* APOLLO *who backs off at
great speed. The projection of the baby disappears just before*
HERMES *enters.* APOLLO *has retreated almost to the
expedition tent.*)

Hermes, whiz-kid, son of Zeus and Maia,
You're the thief who stole my herd from the byre
and dehorned and degutted they went into your lyre.

HERMES
How can you say that? Herd? Herd? Herd?
I'm only five days old. I've never heard the word.
Until that is you come here and them and holler

48

that I'm the one that stole the cattle of Apollo.
Never heard of 'herd'. No, sorry, pet,
'herd' isn't even in my lexicon yet.
I'm still trying to learn the alphabet.
This is my lyre. This is my invention.
Listen to its magic. Everybody! Pay attention!

(HERMES *begins to play the lyre so beautifully and melodiously that angry* APOLLO *and the threatening, advancing* SATYRS *are charmed into listening. At the end of the recital* APOLLO *is sufficiently charmed to want the lyre in exchange for his cut-up cattle.*)

APOLLO

Fellow immortal, son of Zeus and Maia,
I beg you to teach me the art of the lyre.
This was all fated. I feel that it was meant
to create for my sole use this soothing instrument.

(APOLLO *tries to snatch the lyre from* HERMES.)

HERMES

Gerroff my lyre. I made it. It's mine.

APOLLO

But I'm older than you, and a lot more divine.
Give me your gadget. Be a good boy!
I could give class to your trivial toy.

HERMES

It's boring for a baby in his cradle all day.
I'd go proper potty with no lyre to play.

APOLLO

Let me have your gadget or you'll get a good slap.
That papyrus you're wearing. It's full of warm crap.

49

HERMES

That nymph's too snooty to change a kid's nappy.
I can't help it, can I, if I'm all crappy.

(HERMES *sobs*.)

APOLLO

There, there, little fellow, but you're scarcely fit
to give lyre recitals with pants full of shit.
You're frankly disgusting. I think that the lyre
requires a performer in formal attire.
Change your crappy papyrus while I serenade
these lowly satyrs with the lyre you made.

(*Prepares to play and as he plucks the lyre he hears one of his lost cows in the seven strings.*)

[1] Pluck . . . Κανελλω μου . . .
[2] Pluck . . . Παρδαλω μου . . .
[3] Pluck . . . Αρχονρα μου . . .
[4] Pluck . . . Αστηρης μου . . .

[5] Pluck . . . Ασπουλα μου . . .
[6] Pluck . . . Λενιω μου . . .
[7] Pluck . . . Μαρυουλα μου . . .

(*The* μου/*moo at the end of each name is echoed by 'mooings' in the air.*)

The elements that made our drama live
might seem, on first appearance, negative.
Deserts, a papyrus torn to tatters,
theft, a trail of turds, and sniffing satyrs . . .
From that unpromising, unlikely start
from barrenness and turds we have brought art,
and art that draws together and transcends
the boundaries of nations and makes friends.
This mottled tortoise, this creeping thing

joined to my cattle makes dumb Nature sing.
Some comfort, maybe, knowing that my herd's
gone into a gadget more soothing than mere words.
Debeeved, bereaved, I almost can rejoice
that was dead and dumb now has a voice.

The gods decreed a fixed scale in creation
from the Olympian, like me, to the crustacean,
and almost at the bottom of the scale,
even below your sort with hoof and tail,
and tail-bearers with no part human, come
creatures like this tortoise who are dumb.
The scale of creation like a scale with notes
runs the whole gamut from gods to goats,
and distinctly closer to the latter,
low on the scale of being, comes the satyr,
earthbound in the way you dance and drink,
goatish in your instinct and your stink.
You're almost at the bottom but not quite.
Below the beasts, all beast, come beetles and the mite
whose mandibles make meals of Sophocles
and leave gaping holes in such lost plays as these.
This little mite, the lowest in creation
turns Sophocles to dust and defecation,
and turns manuscripts of Mankind's masterpieces
to little microbe meals and microbe faeces,
letters, then a line, a page of words
made minutest mincemeat and the tiniest of turds.
The gods decreed that transformation
was a basic principle in all creation.
The preferred direction's lower into higher
like the tortoise turned into this lyre,
a process that the desert mite reverses
every time he snacks on buried verses.

CHORUS OF SATYRS

I

It's very sad, though, the tortoise had to die.

As part goat or horse, I part identify.

2

When Nature gets made use of for Man's needs
my heart, at least the horse part of me, bleeds.

3

But when I see the outcome, all the rest
of me, the two-thirds human, is impressed.

4

One part wonders. One part identifies.
And both parts bring the tears into my eyes.

5

I greet the gadget of the gutted shell
but grieve for the deroofed animal as well.

6

We've got hoofs of horn. He might have killed us
and sold our hoofs and guts to banjo-builders.

7

Odd how we're always in things at the start –
the creation of fire, the lyre, wine and art.

8

We're envoys of Nature who give their consent
to surrender the substance they use to invent.

9

Woodlands for barbecues, pressed grapes for wine
but where should a satyr start drawing the line?

10

Since fire first came to earth the charcoal-makers
have bulldozed down Arcadia's bosky acres.

11

The leafy bushes we used to quaff and screw in
the barbecuing craze brought into ruin.

12

The dryads undergo decortication
and retreat from reservation to reservation.

1

Always in retreat, moved on yet again
outside the pale of lyre-playing men.

2

They're encouraged by the consent of us man/horses
in their exploitation of Earth's natural resources.

3

Ay, and I ought to confess to being a quick consentor
to grapes being crushed for wine by its inventor.

4

When Dionysos started giving wine away
the horse part of the satyr never said *neigh*.

5

Witnessing wine, I formed the intention
of witnessing every year its re-invention.

APOLLO

And soon you'll be free to drink till you fall,
the freedom it seems that you want most of all.
But first let's find a name to honour the creatures
who died to give the lyre its essential features.
The cattle and the tortoise that had to die
should give this thing a name we'll call it by.
The future should be able to deduce
its animal origin from χελων and βους
To honour gut and shell that give its tone

53

I hereby call this thing the *boucelloniphone*.

CHORUS OF SATYRS

1

But we should honour more than these two.
What about us satyrs who ran it to ground?

2

We're allus excluded when t'honours come round.

3

What about *satyro*boucelloniphone?

APOLLO

*Apollo*satyroboucelloniphone!

SILENUS
(*suddenly appearing but as though he'd been there all the time*)

Apollo*sileno*satyroboucellon-
and-all-the-bloody-rest-i-phone!

APOLLO

Let's go back to 'lyre' and forget the whole zoo.
And *now* the reward that I promised you.
A reward for you satyrs and for you lot out there
is to listen to the lyre's world première.

(APOLLO *takes up the lyre and plays a beautiful melody.
The* SATYRS *are genuinely and deeply enraptured by the
melody. So much so that when* APOLLO *has finished his recital
the* SATYRS *crowd round and want to have a turn with the
instrument.*)

SATYR I

Oh, it's wonderful. Let me have a go!
I'd love to try it out.

54

(*Suddenly very angry*)

NO! NO! NO!

My advice is stick to being satyrs
and don't go meddling with musical matters.
You don't need lyres. You're natural celebrators
stuck between animal and human status.
You need no consolations of high art –
your human pain's cancelled by your horse/goat part.
You don't need lyres. Your days proceed
from one need satisfied to the next need.
And because, as satyrs, you're grossly oversexed
the next succeeds the next succeeds the next.
The gratification of all sensual need,
the horny stallion and the randy steed,
the rhythm of your hoofs, your stamp and strut,
have no need of these seven strings of gut.
You're satyrs, remember. You don't need lyres
while your goat parts tether you to brute desires.
When the man part of you feels a human pain
the goat part puts you on your hoofs again.
When a satyr's human part feels human woes
the gee-gee in him just gees up and goes.
Your capers and your clogs' staccato clatters –
exactly the racket expected of satyrs.

I'm Apollo, inspirer, appreciator
of artist, musician and creator.
Tell the truth it didn't suit a god
the cowpoke's lariat and cattle prod.
I'm not a cowherd really. It's more me
the sphere of music and of poetry.
This is now *my* lyre and I define
its music as half-human, half-divine.
And satyrs, I repeat, must not aspire
in any way to mastering my lyre.

Do you need reminding how I had to flay
your brother Marsyas *pour encourager*
and I hereby have to warn all *les autres*
not to touch or try playing one note.

(*The* SATYRS, *already saddened both by the melody and then
by* APOLLO*'s speech, are totally terrified and devastated by his
reminding them of Marsyas, the satyr flayed alive by* APOLLO
*for mastering the flute, newly invented then discarded by
Athene.*)

But I have to grant that you sniffed out the track
and got me what's left of my cattle back.
You kept your promise. My cattle got tracked.
You'll get what I promised as per our pact –
gold and freedom. You're free, if you stay
within the strict form of the satyr play.
Gold and freedom – here's gold. And you're free
so long as you stay here in Arcady.

(APOLLO *plays his lyre while* KYLLENE *comes from the tent
and hands out large gold bars, one to each* SATYR.)

So much for you lot. And as for me
I'm a god, and I'll always be free.
I'm off to compose a new paean or ode
in my very own temple just down the road.

(*Exit* APOLLO *to the Temple of Apollo.* APOLLO *makes the
long exit towards the rear screen with the projection of Apollo
from the Delphi plate now plus the lyre. The* CHORUS OF
SATYRS *are thoroughly cowed. They line up for the 'rewards'
of gold which* APOLLO *had pulled out of a crate. They are like
children lining up for Santa Claus only they have no excitement
at what they receive. Each of the 'gold bars' is in fact a
'ghetto-blaster' wrapped in gold foil. The* SATYRS *sit in a curve
following the rim of the stadium and open their 'presents' in a
half-hearted, sad way, and grumbling as they do. When they*

56

open them they have no idea what they are. The confrontation is
like one of those supposedly amusing accounts of say, Africans
or Indians first seeing some gadget of 'white man's civilization',
and sometimes they are like Cheetah in the Tarzan films getting
hold of a camera, or mirror or telephone.)

CHORUS OF SATYRS

1

Who wants some stupid tortoise to strum?

2

He can stick his bloody banjo up his bum!

3

Once it gains a foothold in our habitat
with its plinkety-plonk, well, that'll be that.

4

It'll be in t'woods, in t'hills, grass, t'air –

5

Ay, even in t'toilet and that's everywhere.

6

Every cave, every grot, every bosky retreat
'll soon be throbbing with Apollo's lyre beat.

7

Plucking piped out from morn till eve.
Here'll be unliveable. We'll all have to leave.

8

There'll be no stretch of sky, no bit of ground
that won't in the end be full of its sound.

9

When Hermes took cow-gut and tortoise-shell
did he know that he'd turn our peace into hell?

You watch what'll happen. It'll force the poor birds
out of business. You mark my words.

As songsters that is. It'll still be their fate
to stew in rich sauces for some human's plate.

It'll usurp the susurrations . . .

                The who?

The rustles, the whispers, the tu-whit and tu-whoo.

The repertoire of rapture, the moan
of doves, the murmur of innumerable bees.

The rustling of dresses of dryades,
their stockingtops purring as their thighs
rub together . . .

          the buzz of bluebottles and flies.

Ay, birdsong's *passé*. This lyre'll usurp.
the song of the skylark, the cricket's chirp.

Eventually everything's going to get drowned
in such all-surrounding and man-made sound.

Don't like it at all. It'll come to no good
letting such loud din loose in the wood.

This lyre contraption's the thin end of the wedge.
We'll soon have this Muzak behind every hedge.

The beginning of the end. You wait and see,
There'll be plinkety-plonk from every damned tree.

(*By this time the* CHORUS OF SATYRS *have opened all their
'presents'. The ghetto-blasters lie on the ground in front of them
forming a curve. Suddenly, very loudly, the ghetto-blasters begin
to play the same melody as* APOLLO *played during his lyre
recital, but deafening rock-style. The* SATYRS *try to dance to it,
can't and in a panic at the sound they flee to the rear screen.*
SILENUS *is left alone to face the unbearable chorus of ghetto-
blasters. One by one he smashes them into silence. When the
echoes have died away he speaks seriously to the audience.*)

SILENUS

Civilization! Once man starts on that track
even for a satyr there's no going back.
The 'boucelloniphone', Apollo's lyre
leads, by leaps and bounds, to the amplifier,
the guts of cows and the tortoise-shell
to steel-plucked deafening decibel.

(*Lights a brazier and wraps a papyrus 'cloak' round himself.*)

Papyrus to codex, book to film and tape
once they're invented then there's no escape.
And fire, that takes the bleak chill off the night
could, if men don't watch it, set the world alight.
Disco descends directly from his lyre
and global holocaust from cosy fire.

The glowing grills where *kokkoretsi* turns
grow to conflagrations where the whole globe burns.

(*Looks, finds the moon.*)

The moon hymned for aeons by love-sick hacks
is already pock-marked with spaceboot tracks.
Tracks no earthbound, earth-loving satyr wants to
    follow
though that waste above's been visited by Apollo.
When the world seems hurtling in the wrong direction
remember the satyr with his wineskin and erection.

(*Regards his own limp appendage.*)

Sorry to say so but that's a side
of satyrdom the lads have to provide.
My time for tupping's done as you can see.
No maenad's moist μουνάκι opens now for me.

But a satyr, good people, doesn't just exist
solely for fucking or for getting pissed.
We're not just the clowns sent in to clear the ring
we're here to show surprise at everything.
We satyrs are on hand to reassess
from basic principles all you possess,
to show reactions apparently naive
to what you take for granted or believe.
To ask the simple wherefore, why, and what,
to show, for the first time ever, fire's hot.
We're sort of guinea-pigs for gadgets, fire,
the sculptural likeness, this new-fangled lyre.
Of all the gadgets we were required to test
this gadget made from grape juice suits me best.

We're all served our time with that weight on our heads
But no satyr ever trod where tragedy treads
Gods, kings, and heroes have all walked there.

High and low divided just by a stair
Now's my big chance! Do I dare, do I dare!

(*Spotlight on papyrus.*)

> . . . ως απολλυμαι κακως . . . O woe, O woe.

(*Enter* SILENUS *through papyrus.*)

Not bad for a satyr for his first go!

Satyrs in theatre are on hand to reassess
doom and destiny and dire distress.
Six hours of tragedy and half an hour of fun.
But they were an entity conceived as one.
But when the teachers and critics made their selections
they elbowed the satyrs with embarrassing erections.
Those teachers of tragedy sought to exclude
the rampant half-animals as offensive and rude.
But whose eyes first beheld the Promethean blaze?

(*In answer comes the shouted response of the* CHORUS OF
SATYRS *supported also by the 'ghosts' of the 8000 spectators at
the ancient Pythian Games.*)

CHORUS

Ours!

SILENUS

(*Shouting back*)

And whose horse-lugs hear the first lyre when it plays?

CHORUS

Ours!

SILENUS

And who kissed the flames and found they were hot?

CHORUS

US!

SILENUS

And who saw their ugly mugs first fashioned in pot?

CHORUS

US!

SILENUS

And when the first vintage was picked from the vine,
Who watched it ferment, who supped the first wine?

CHORUS

US!

SILENUS

Who pioneered the art of getting pissed?

CHORUS

US!

SILENUS

Who's indispensable to the papyrologist?

CHORUS

US!
Ichneftés. Ichneftés. Ichneftés.

SILENUS

Who scrabbled in sand to find bits of Greek?

CHORUS

US!

Who pulled from oblivion the words that we speak?
US! US! US!

US! US! US!

(SILENUS *allows the echoes of the* CHORUS *and the 8000
ghosts of the Pythian Games to die away, then continues.*)

SILENUS

We have to keep a proper distance though.
We're meant as Calibans to serve a Prospero.
Deferential, rustic, suitably in awe
of new inventions is what your satyr's for.
But we mustn't, as you heard, actually aspire
to actually *play* your actual lyre.
Wondering, applauding, that's our participation
but satyrs have to stick to their satyr station.
Apollo mentioned Marsyas who lost his skin
and all he really wanted was to join in.
Did Marsyas deserve his awful flaying
for a bit of innocent *aulos* playing?
Your satyr's fine in music just as long
he doesn't think that *he* can sing the song.
To be an applauding punter but not to trespass
on cultural preserves like brother Marsyas.

The *aulos* was Athene's flute. She flung it away
so why shouldn't my brother pick it up and play?
After only a few blows the goddess gave the flute
she'd just invented the elegant boot.
She flung the thing aside. Do you know why?
Think of the *aulos*. Ever had a try?
You puff your cheeks out, like this, when you play
and *she* didn't like her face to look that way.

63

She though it unattractive. Well, its true
her cheeks looked like balloons when the goddess blew.
And who should see the flung flute in the grass
but our brother satyr, Marsyas?
Questions of cosmetics scarcely matter
to one who had the ugly mug of a satyr.

It wasn't for good looks that Marsyas was noted
so he blew and blew and let his cheeks get bloated.
He took himself off to a quiet bit of wood
and girned and puffed and grunted and got *good*.
Can't you hear the Muses on Parnassós say
'Who gave a common satyr licence to play?'
Music's an inner circle that has to exclude
from active participation a beast so crude.

'How can *he* be a virtuoso on the flute?
Look at the hoofs on him. He's half a brute!'
His one and only flaw. He showed that flutes
sound just as beautiful when breathed into by 'brutes'.
It confounded the categories of high and low
when Caliban could outplay Prospero.

So the goddess Athene's discarded whistle
turned brother Marsyas to gore and gristle.
And while Marsyas suffered his slow flaying
Apollo looked on with his 'doo-dah' playing.
The last thing that he saw was his own skin
like a garment at his feet with no one in.
Wherever the losers and the tortured scream
the lyres will be playing the Marsyas theme.
You'll hear the lyres playing behind locked doors
where men flay their fellows for an abstract cause.
The kithara cadenza, the Muse's mezzo trill
cover the skinning and the screaming still.

Wherever in the world there is prison and pain
the powerful are playing the Marsyas refrain.

In every dark dungeon where blood has flowed
the lyre accompanies the Marsyas ode.
Wherever the racked and the anguished cry
there's always a lyre-player standing by.
Some virtuoso of Apollo's *Ur*-violin
plays for the skinners as they skin.

And *why* shouldn't Marsyas or me aspire
to be virtuosos of the flute or . . . lyre?

If Marsyas had touched it and said 'ooo'
the way that us satyrs are supposed to do,
but he went and picked it up and blew the flute
and that was trespassing for the man/brute.
For *them* it would have been quite enough
to have given it just one abortive puff,
a buffoonish ballooning of the brutish cheeks
producing a few, and inexpert, squeaks,
that would have amused them and been OK
but Marsyas, man/animal, he learned to *play*.
To have watched him smell it, test it with his teeth
or use it like the pygmies as a penis sheath,
all allowable, all tolerated fun,
but the Apollonian goes for his gun,
when it suddenly dawns on him the swine
the pearl is cast before by one divine
knows it's a pearl, and not some novel food
and aspires beyond dumb swinetude.
When he enters the Culture it represents
they reach for their skin-removing instruments.

They're less accommodating the satyrs of today.
They wouldn't condescend to be in a satyr play.
They've joined the *polis* and they've learned its ways
but they despise its music and its plays.
I'm too used to it here. I'll never lead 'em
into the future with their new-found freedom.
I want to implore them: 'Children, stay

and be satyrs with me and play out this play.'

But they won't listen, and they're on their way
straight through the confines of the stupid satyr play.

(*Enter the new generation of* SATYRS. *They are like football
hooligans with scarves, flags, etc., and chanting and clapping.
The* SATYRS *spray the name 'Marsyas' (in Greek letters:
Μαρσυασ) first with red, then with white aerosol paints, the
colour of the Greek team Olympiakos. Then they add Μαρσυασ
in blue for England. ('Marsyas! Marsyas! Marsyas!') They slash
the papyrus. They spray Μαρσυασ in inflammable fuel and set
light to it so that the name of Μαρσυασ blazes on the screen
papyrus. They kick the smashed ghetto-blasters into life. They
blare out the 'Marsyas Theme'.*)

That's enough, lads. Leave things as they are.
I may be a satyr. But in there I'm star.

CHORUS OF SATYRS
(*Passing along a torch lit from* SILENUS' *brazier and cans of
beer.*)

1
We were the witnesses when the first fire came.

2
We were the first to flinch from the flame.

3
When I kissed the fire it blistered my face.

4
I burned my beard off in that fiery embrace.

5
Yer, we thought the flames lovely and gave 'em a kiss.

6

And our beards set alight with a blistering hiss.

7

They used our innocence to play a bad joke.

8

Ever since then my hair's smelled of smoke.

9

It's not just that fact that Marsyas got flayed.

10

There's plenty of tricks the buggers have played.

11

And we connived at the clowning, thought it a way
of getting a hoofhold into a play.

12

We're going to destroy and we're enjoying

1

destroying for the sake of destroying.

2

We're doing the burning, and the bloody lyre
is wired to our turned-up amplifier.

(*Loud beat from ghetto-blaster.*)

3

No more deferential dummies from a satyr play.
From now on MARSYAS RULES OK?

(*Ghetto-blaster beat.*)

If I can't be a man I'll be wholly goat

and stuff the papyrus down Sophocles' throat.

(*Ghetto-blaster beat.*)

4
Fellaheen, phallus-bearers only for farce.
Well, show us a tragedy we'll show you our arse.

5
Aeschylus, Sophocles, gerroff our backs.
We're hijacking Culture and leaving no tracks.

(*The* SATYR *begin to burn down the papyrus of the* Ichneutae.)

SILENUS
Don't burn the papyrus. That's where we come from!

(*They watch the papyrus burn and drink beer and scatter the cans
on the mounds where the papyri were extracted from. These are
the new rubbish mounds of Oxyrhynchus.*)

To them old Silenus is an Uncle Tom.

(*Shouting to* SATYRS)

Don't burn the papyrus. We're all inside.
Don't burn the papyrus. It's satyricide!

CHORUS OF SATYRS
Either fuck off, old feller, or give us a hand.

(SILENUS *stays still.*)
Then fuck off, old feller, back to fairyland.

SILENUS
Apollo promised freedom. And free you now are
but Apollo didn't intend it to go so far.

(*Begins to exit, then stops.*)

> I didn't mind a bit of inferior status
> as long as there was Bacchus to inebriate us.
> I didn't mind a bit of lowly forelock-tugging
> as long as it went with retsina-glugging.
> To social inequality I turned a blind eye
> if that guaranteed the liquor supply.
> Some sort of pattern seemed to exist,
> get a bit pissed on then go and get pissed.
> I didn't mind conniving with gods and their greed
> if my modest wants were guaranteed.
> Unlike my poor flayed brother, Marsyas,
> I never yearned to move out of my class.
> Better we satyrs stay where we are
> with Bacchus at least there's a buckshee bar.

(SILENUS *tries to drink again from his wineskin and finds it empty. He begins to pick over the rubbish mounds for discarded beer cans.*)

> I'm a happy horse/human, half and half.
> Maybe I'd like less hair on my calf,
> my features might be a little less coarse
> more of the human and less of the horse.
> But unlike brother Marsyas I don't aspire
> to master the flute or play on the lyre.
> In short, I suppose, I'm not really averse
> to being a satyr. I could do a lot worse.

(*To* CHORUS)

> So don't make waves, boys. Don't rock the boat.
> And add up the pluses of being man/goat.

(*The* CHORUS OF SATYRS *take no notice, and go about their destruction and scattering of litter.*)

69

My lads, they're different. They don't agree.
When they call for freedom. They mean *really* free.

(SILENUS *makes a long exit to where the rear screen used to*
hang. The destroyed papyri leave two 'goal posts' and the
CHORUS OF SATYRS *begin a six-aside football match. They*
use a rolled-up bundle of papyrus of the Ichneutae *as their ball,*
and then it changes into a real football. The cheer of the ancient
8000 ghosts of the Pythian Games is heard when a goal is scored.
Also earlier chants. We hear again the fragments that began the
play, APOLLO*'s first words and the first words of the whole play*
now going back into oblivion.)

VOICE OF APOLLO

. . . .]σ[. . .

. . . .]κιο[. . .

. . . .]πειτα[. . .

. . . .]πεσσυϑ[. . .

. . .]γ[. . .]λ[. . . . . .]ω[. . .

(*The final omega is echoed with a huge 'Oh' from the 8000 ghosts*
at the Pythian Games. There is the sound like a dying firework of
Ιχνευτες *off the Phaedriades.*)

(*After the darkness for the curtain call the* CHORUS *run from the rear screen with blazing torches and a flaming 'World Cup' which is placed centre stadium. They then rush forward with torches high and reprise the 'Paean for the People of Delphi', but this time it is 'sung' not rhythmically chanted.*

They hand their torches to the 'Greek Fellaheen'.

Eight members of the CHORUS *pick up eight scattered crate lids and hold them up to the audience. They are the eight letters of the name of* ΣΟΦΟΚΛΗΣ *but in the wrong order. The remaining four* CHORUS *reprise a little of the clog dance.*

GRENFELL *and* HUNT *enter from the rear screen with electric torches searching.*

With the help of the audience they rearrange the letters held up by the CHORUS *so that they read the name of Sophocles.*

ΣΟΦΟΚΛΗΣ

This is the curtain call of Sophocles.

APPENDIX

The text of *The Trackers of Oxyrhynchus* presents a composer with an unconventional set of parameters. Finding musical solutions to the problems of a chanting crowd of ghosts haunting the ancient Pythian Games stadium; a chorus of Satyrs whose clog-shod feet demand an extra rhythmical dimension and the fact that only pitchless material can exist prior to the invention of the first pitched instrument, the lyre, two-thirds of the way into the work, necessitates the use of unconventional means.

I chose to compose an electro-acoustic score which made use of treated digital recordings of fragments of text, woven together with percussive sounds. These were triggered 'live' by the performers with their hands, feet or voices. I was able to use the Phaedriades as a huge reverberation chamber which allowed for the sounds of the actual performance to become sufficiently delayed and magnified to provide a constantly changing accompaniment to the ongoing performance.

The music was written during a four-week rehearsal period at the National Theatre Studio and all actors and musicians learnt the material by rote as it evolved. As a consequence, very little of the score performed in Delphi was written down. However, 'Pindar's Hymn' and 'The Tracking Satyrs' Dance' were notated for this publication in order to give a more complete record of the one performance we gave in the ancient Pythian Games stadium in Delphi.

S. Edwards

PINDAR'S HYMN

S.EDWARDS

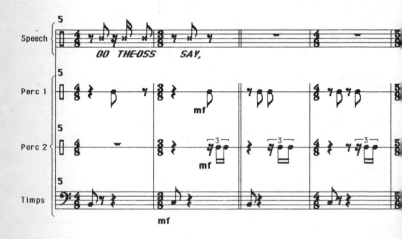

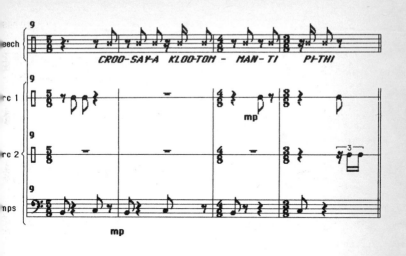

CROO-SAY-A KLOO-TOM - MAN-TI PI-THI

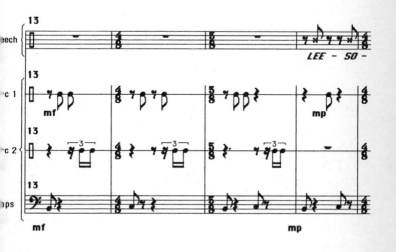

LEE - SO -

77

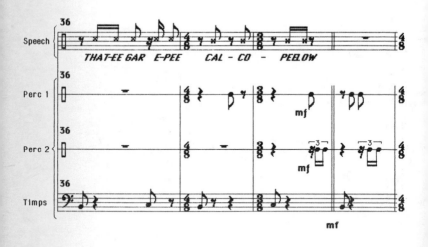

78

PSOFONAH-EE-ON   CA-STA-

mp

mp

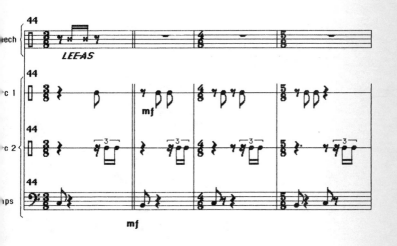

LEE-AS

mf

mf

A-MAH - CA - NEE - AHN   A-LEX-OON   TE-

EE-SIN E-MES   TE   TEE - MESS

THE TRACKING SATYRS' DANCE

S. EDWARDS

82

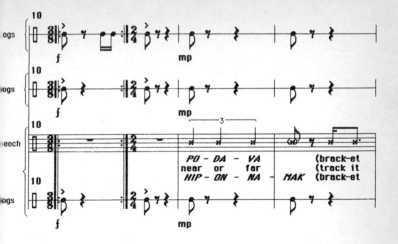

83

84

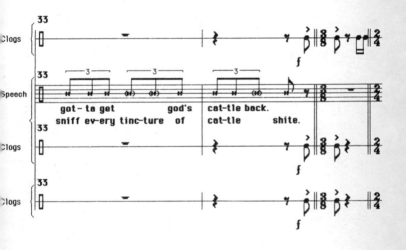

85

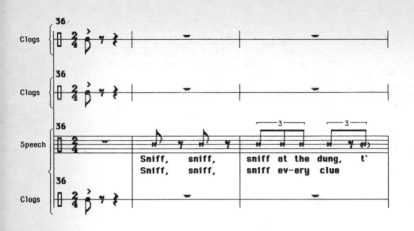

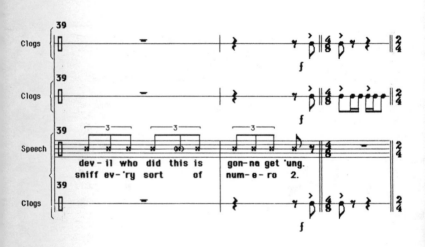

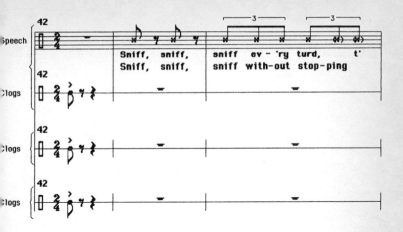

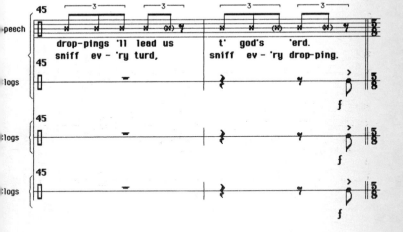

89

90

91

92

force has sent us out of our minds.

Cows don't moo from their be-hinds.

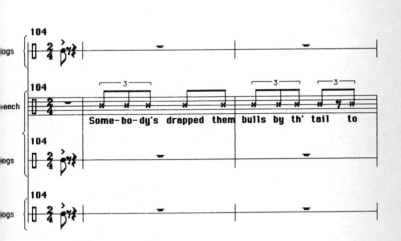

Some-bo-dy's drapped them bulls by th' tail to

94

Grenfell (Jack Shepherd) and Hunt (Barrie Rutter) sorting
papyri in front of the expedition tent

Kyllene (Juliet Stevenson)

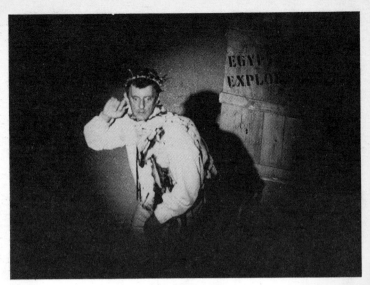

Apollo (Jack Shepherd)

Satyrs burst out of the Egypt Exploration Fund crates
(performance 12 July 1988)

The Satyrs cavort

Rehearsals, Ancient Stadium of Delphi